Danger Wall May Fall

LYNN LURIA-SUKENICK

Danger Wall May Fall

SHORT STORIES

ZOLAND BOOKS
Cambridge, Massachusetts

First edition published in 1997 by
Zoland Books, Inc.
384 Huron Avenue
Cambridge, Massachusetts 02138
Copyright © 1997 by Paul Luria

FIRST EDITION

Book design by Boskydell Studio

Printed in the United States of America

04 03 02 01 00 99 98 97   8 7 6 5 4 3 2 1

This book is printed on acid-free paper, and its binding
materials have been chosen for strength and durability.

Library of Congress Cataloging-in-Publication Data
Luria-Sukenick, Lynn.
Danger wall may fall: stories / by Lynn Luria-Sukenick. — 1st ed.
p.   cm.
ISBN 0-944072-76-3 (alk. paper)
I. Title
PS3569.U3D36   1997
813'.54 — dc21   96-37562   CIP

ACKNOWLEDGMENTS

"After the Rains Only the Shadow Knows" in *New Letters*.
"Still Life with Bath" in *The Massachusetts Review* and
in the anthology *Lovers* (Crossing Press). "Falling" in the
anthology *Breaking Up Is Hard To Do* (Crossing Press).
"Under Malathion" in *Sonora Review* and in the
anthology *In Celebration of the Muse* (M Press).
"The Man with the Blues Guitar" in *Fiction International*.
"Do You Know the Facts of Life? (Quiz)" in *Yellow Silk*,
the anthologies *Yellow Silk* (Crown) and
Touching Fire (Carrol & Graf).

Contents

Danger Wall May Fall

Introduction

HEREWITH Lynn Luria-Sukenick's bittersweet, knowing, vivid short fictions. Those who knew Lynn personally will be reminded of how cruelly early her death came, and of the singularity of the voice it silenced. Those acquainted with Lynn's poetry will not be surprised to find reflected in these stories the same grace and lyrical focus characteristic of her poems — but there is more, here.

Each of these stories presents and illuminates one sort of aftermath or another. In fact, Lynn could be described justly as a specialist in aftermaths, in the poetics of aftermaths. Each account takes place after the fact — post-flood, post-marriage, post-woman's conference, post-affair, post-earthquake. Reading Lynn's stories all in a row, and absorbing her backward-looking reflective-analytical approach as I went along, faux aphorisms in the style of Chamfort or Joubert came to me . . . along the lines of *Life, largely a succession of aftermaths*. And that happened, I think, in response to a pressure in these stories themselves, whose narrators struggle over and over to deal productively with bad luck, to reframe or compress resentments and disappointments into silver bullets, neo-aphorisms, useful maxims. On living in California, one character observes to herself *Memory isn't* essential, but you really have to have a car. At another point: *I'm afraid of the future because I'm losing my memory . . . Soon you'll start looking old, then you'll always be in a bad mood. What was the chemistry of self-pity and what could you eat to change it?* the same character wonders. And: *There was only one thing worse than the end and that was the beginning of the end.* Now these are not classic, fully-achieved one-two punch epigrams or aphorisms. But they constitute brilliant examples of self-talk aspiring toward, driven toward, the kinds of closure that art, in the form of the perfect epigram, among other forms, can yield.

Ultimately, these stories are about consolation, and as studies of the varieties of consolation, they go very deep. I don't know that the mechanics of consolation have ever been delineated at such fine resolution. Many of the generic obstacles to consolation are dealt with, frontally or obliquely — aging, natural disasters, loneliness, feminine disadvantage. And the classic maneuvers toward securing consolation — with the exception of recourse to religion — are performed by Lynn's narrators, including the resort to the aesthetic, to nature, to remembering the good times. I think I see an elusive progress through these stories, from the dark conclusions of "Under Malathion," through the sardonica of "Do You Know the Facts of Life? (Quiz)," to the nuanced acceptance of things as they are in "What is Lost, What is Missing, What is Gone: Scenes After the Earthquake," which was one of the last things she wrote.

As serious as the underlying thematic of Lynn's tales may be, it would be wrong to picture this work as grimly didactic. It isn't. Humor and wit are present throughout. "Please become seated," says the receptionist in a doctor's office, straining toward the genteel. Locale is always sensuously constructed for the reader. You always know where you are, physically, tactilely, as you read. And the reproduction of the atmosphere and mores of late twentieth-century Santa Cruz is consummate, embodying Lynn's friendly ambivalence — if that's the right formulation — toward the peculiar place that became her home. Lynn's ear for dialogue is keen. And although the stories are outwardly conventional in form (with a couple of exceptions), that's deceptive. Looked at closely, the stories represent compromises between the opposed impulses — within Lynn — toward expressive spontaneity and toward fidelity to classic form . . . jazz versus the well-tempered clavier, shouts and imprecations versus the mantra, unharnessed inward self-examination versus the epigram. *The work of an author who knows too well what literature should be makes me think of the handwriting of a man who knows graphology* is an aphorism of Jean Rostand's that comes to mind because it points so directly at what Lynn's fiction is not.

My friendship with Lynn began in the 1950s, after her marriage to my college classmate Ron Sukenick. Our friendship was of a particular kind. It took place in visits and phone conversations — rarely in letters — at widely separated intervals. We never hung out. Living, as we did, always at opposite sides of the country, or even in different countries, hanging out wasn't a possibility. Lynn was an early partisan of my writing (my first published story was one she placed in *Epoch*) and I admired her poetry (beginning with the Houdini suite). As writers, we had a common defect — a self-defeating sort of perfectionism — which we criticized in one another to no great effect. Our friendship was about writing, books, the literary scene, unappreciated writers we had discovered (Douglas Woolf was a great favorite of hers). We seemed quickly, in our contacts, to get up to date on what was going on personally, and then to move on into intense and kind of exhausting literary conversation. She was an inspired conversationalist, always colorful, always managing in some way to be both provocative and judicious. And she did judge. That was a part of her character, and it arose from her ferocious attachment to art. She was an absolutist when it came to art. It was

bracing to talk to Lynn, whose opinions and quibbles and pro-
nunciamentos stayed with me, generating unasked-for internal
arguments long after she'd left town.

We didn't talk extensively about one another's work, at least
not until she'd diverged from poetry to begin writing fiction, rel-
atively late in her career. I didn't see myself as useful to her on the
subject of poetry, given that my own ideas on poetry were and
are so restrictive and idiosyncratic, if not actually peculiar. Of
her work in performance art, I knew very little, partly, no doubt,
because I was not temperamentally very positive about the genre.
Lynn was, as so many of her students have told me, a masterly
teacher of writing, but I missed seeing her in action.

The hard part of Lynn's life, after her divorce from Ron, and
after a shocking "tenurectomy" (as she called it) at the University
of California at Santa Cruz, coincided with her turn toward fiction. She focused with even more concentration on fiction during her time at the University of California at San Diego and into
the period of her final struggle with cancer. Not all of her last fic-
tional projects are represented here, since many of them were left
unfinished at the time of her death at the age of fifty-seven. I
urged her to write fiction, and to write in longer forms. The work
presented displays excellently the powers she deployed as a fiction writer, her technical skills, her command of recollected experience, her dark wit. A novel was in progress as her illness
worsened, but dying well, as she did, took all her strength.

Norman Rush
July 1996

After the Rains Only the Shadow Knows

S HE WAS AT THE CAFE DOMANI, a haven of ferns and oak tables tucked into a courtyard behind the tree-lined mall in downtown Santa Cruz. The ceiling fan turned lazily above her as she bent her head over the horoscopes in the *Santa Cruz Local,* the paper laid out next to her morning mail — a water bill from Valley Water and a letter from her mother saying that her father still had the water around his heart, though he had not grown significantly worse; they were in the Adirondacks near a quiet lake. She searched the Virgo segment, lit up by a neat square of sunlight from the window, for some word about her father, some clue about her future:

> This is a week in which you can water down impending losses by grounding yourself in the earthly gains of the past. The water stored in your eighth house can be released if you take for yourself the unaccustomed privilege of seeing in the dark. Don't count on love to keep you dry.

She reread the horoscope and fished out a Kleenex. Just after her lover had told her he was planning to see other women again she had gotten a cold, her body choosing this instead of fits of crying. Her voice was already pretty hoarse, and she had to be on the local radio station at four o'clock, to be interviewed by the Poetry Brothers. The cafe's radio was turned to the station she would be talking on in a couple of hours, and she recognized an aria from *Don Giovanni*.

She went back to the paper and checked her lover's horoscope: Each week she watched for the blends and mutual insinuations of their signs, her Virgo earth and his Aries fire. She looked up his rising sign as well; he always consulted both because he was a twin, like her father, and used to two of everything, or so she supposed. She pressed an acupressure point on the outside of her wrist, the point for calm. Then she read the letter again, a reassuring letter that frightened her, and placed it over Virgo so that it caught the sun.

The sun had been out for a week now, following the long heavy rains that came after the January flood, when weather and news had become the same in Santa Cruz and in her town up in the mountains. Every once in a while in the recent months it had seemed to threaten news but then just hung over everyone like weather. They had said that kind of storm could happen only once a century. Yet a few miles from her house there was still the danger of mudslides, the earth so soaked with rain that another inch might push the mountains into motion again.

She switched to her left wrist. The day of the flood had given everyone the feeling that they had a story, that was the only good thing that had come from it. Everyone, she thought, needed a story and someone to tell it to. The best people to tell these stories to were the ones who had imagined them beforehand — this was called love. It was essential to have a second story these days, however, since love didn't last and you might be trapped in a flood. Her lover had no story about why he hadn't called during the flood, could not explain the giant *no* inside his regard for her; and she didn't question him, although it stunned her that he hadn't called. Maybe because he was a twin he thought that everything happened twice, that there was always another chance. She pressed harder and concentrated on the *chi* traveling from her sacrum down the back of each leg.

There had been ten dead in her town after the flood — a woman swept from a bridge into the churning brown river while her sweetheart reached for her too late, another couple locked in a last embrace on their bed under seventy feet of mud. Dozens of houses on Love Creek had collapsed; nine people had died there. Stay out of love, she thought — the toxins in Love Canal, the flash flood in Loveland, Colorado, that had killed one hundred people. When a flood came you were supposed to go two by two. But while the hills were sliding and uprooted redwoods were hurtling down the river in his direction her lover was safe in town hugging his slide guitar, playing, "Two trains runnin' down that line. One's my friend, the other's a friend of mine." She had never understood that song.

She put one finger on her upper lip and the other hand on top of her head, the points for shock. The whole city had been in a state of shock since the flood. And many people with heart conditions had died, although they had not been counted as casualties.

She was worried about her father, back in New York; his heart had grown weaker since the death of her uncle Arthur over a year ago. What she really wanted to talk about on the radio was her father, radio and her father — how when she was eight he had bought her a small white radio because she had conjunctivitis and couldn't see. Long before she was born, he had been a writer for the Fred Allen Show, Ipana and Sal Hepatica, then later for Jack Benny, Jell-O then Lucky Strike. Before she was six, she had learned most of the jokes in their repertoires, had loved her father's kidding around, even though she would sometimes plead, "No, Daddy, *really.*"

She took her hands away from her face; a couple of people were looking at her. The felicities of *Don Giovanni* went to wherever music goes when it's over and were replaced by a familiar toccata and fugue, pumping through the air, searching as a fugue is always searching. The sunlight crept away from her mother's letter and settled on a jelly glass filled with speckled Peruvian lilies. She did the acupressure point for colds discreetly, one hand holding the side of her neck, the other pressing up under her collarbone. Then she took out a pocket mirror to check on the redness of her nose. At least on the radio you didn't have to smile. Her good-looking lover was a mirror twin, left-handed, with a right-handed twin who parted his hair on the opposite side. She herself was left-handed. She had heard that every left-handed person had been a twin once, in the very earliest stages of life, gastula, blastula, the partner lost in the fetus' insufficient commitment to cell division.

If the Poetry Brothers asked her for her flood story she would tell them that in a disaster the safest place is your radio. The rain had begun at night; like childbirth, had gone on and on, and by morning her road was unpassable: Three new lakes lay between her and the highway. Her electric stove and heaters were dead. She climbed under all the blankets she had, huddled there rigid with cold, and listened to KGO as it inundated her with bulletin after bulletin: The Golden Gate Bridge was closed; the freeways were waterlogged; the hills of Marin were sliding. Then the hills in Ben Lomond were going too, only a mile away, people fleeing the homes that had started to slip down saturated hillsides, houses collapsing in a matter of seconds. Either the batteries were weak or she had not been able to get them to touch properly so she strained to hear through a fuzz of static that coated the announcer's voice and obliterated much of what he was saying. Maybe her hills were sliding, too, though she could feel nothing but the cold and could see nothing but sheets of water attacking the window, the same rain that, miles away, was escaping with everyone's belongings, beating everything limp.

While she was straining to listen to the radio she felt blind; she remembered how after the conjunctivitis she would get up in the middle of the night and turn the lights on to make sure she hadn't lost her sight. But the sound of the radio was better than the hemorrhaging silence that filled the room when she turned it off. So she stayed in bed, under a pile of blankets, listening to the radio until nightfall and then, starved, felt her way toward the kitchen, toward the rotting things in the refrigerator, flicking dead light switches, watching the light from her candle run nervously up the walls and crawl out onto the ceiling. He hadn't called, although only two days before he had spent the night there, had lit the candles over dinner and then in the bedroom.

When she pushed up a light switch and nothing happened she had the feeling that her brakes were going, her foot pressing the pedal all the way down, her legs turning to water. She had known he wouldn't stay beyond Sunday morning when she heard him singing in the shower, "Got the key to the highway, Lord, it's time for me to run." She had left the dishes all day Sunday because she liked contemplating the remains of the dinner she'd taken so much trouble to prepare. The sheets smelled of him, his sweat like the deep notes of an organ. But when the rains began the remains were not enough. She couldn't breathe, waiting for him to call, couldn't get warm.

All night there was an eerie steady wind, as the temperature sank. She hadn't fallen asleep until dawn, and then she dreamed he had stayed the night. In the dream he got up early to fry some bacon, she could hear it sizzling while she lingered in bed; then she realized that the sizzle of bacon was actually the crackling of fire creeping under her bedroom door, a door he had locked from the outside as he left. When she woke she heard nothing but the ancient crepitation of rain. Water preceded fire, she thought, and she felt a primeval loneliness and panic, the panic of a creature crouching in the dark with no fire to fend off predators.

It had been raining twenty-three hours when she found his ring on the floor, between the bed and the night table. She put it on the table, close to her, and gazed into the lapis lazuli stone in the flicker of candlelight, pretending it was a magic ring, pretending she could find him in it. She imagined she saw him struggling and she followed the struggle until she saw it was with a woman and then she realized it wasn't a struggle.

The waitress let the check float down onto her table. She glanced at it and then noticed the water bill again: It was a shut-off notice, the deadline today. It was either too much water or not enough. Some things stopped before you wanted them to; others went on longer than you could bear.

On the third day the rains had stopped but the electricity was still not working. He hadn't called. Why hadn't he found her? He could unravel any riddle, get to any place by putting his finger on the map. "Figure this out," she said once. "I said something to the bus driver when I was going to Sunnyvale, expecting the answer three o'clock and instead he said yes, what did I say?"

He thought a minute. "You said, 'Can you tell me when this bus gets to Sunnyvale?'" Even her father hadn't been able to answer that one. So, long after the rains, when they invited her to be on the radio, she asked him, "What was that old joke, no soap, radio?" It was the first joke she'd ever heard, and the first test: If you laughed you were a jerk, if you said you didn't get it you were a jerk. She seemed to remember there was some sexual innuendo in it, a man and a woman, one of them in the bathtub, but no, he insisted it was about penguins on an ice floe. Then he got sidetracked and didn't tell it to her. *No soap,* that was an expression long ago, when her father wrote for radio, meaning *nothing doing.*

The Cafe Domani was filling up and voices climbed the high brick walls like echoing vines. Distortion set in when there were more than a dozen people in the cafe. She gathered up her mail and the newspaper and left two dollars on the table. She would go to Hope's house and find some quiet. She had a key for in-city emergencies, breathers when she didn't feel like driving back up to the mountains.

Her car purred in the sun as she drove along the streets that led from the pier to the top of Beach Hill. The ocean smelled fishy today. Fishy — that meant something suspicious. "You'll never come back," her father had said when she left for California ten years before, and he had been right. To him only the serious buildings of Manhattan were real, but he had heard about the seductions of the other coast, a coast like a beautiful woman holding your face between her hands, her hands lotioned and perfumed.

She pulled up in front of a huge Victorian house whose grandeur had been squelched by a muddy brown paint job. The car ahead of her had a bumper sticker that said, "The Afterlife — Now!" The house, now divided into apartments, had once been pink, the same pink as the boardwalk's cotton candy, but fainter, as if it were fainting backward, like a Victorian lady. As she let herself in she could hear the tiny screams from the roller coaster a block away, the last California amusement park near the ocean.

She hadn't been to Hope's apartment in weeks. The enormous top-floor space had windows that faced in four directions — the roller coaster, the Pacific Ocean, the old motel called El View, and an empty lot filled with sunflowers. She saw out the window that there was someone going into El View who looked a little like her father, the aquiline nose, the bent posture he had acquired in the last few years of heart disease. Her father had painted portraits of men like that until gradually, slowly, he had become one himself, more and more exasperated by the weakness of his heart. Twenty years ago his Sunday painting had expanded to daily painting, to selling his work, having shows. He painted underdogs, indigent men and women with resigned faces, even his portraits of her and her brother looked sad and deprived.

"You're such a funny man," her mother had said. "Why do you

paint such sad people?" He had shrugged. "People are sad," he said. "Why would I bother to be funny unless people were sad?"

The phone rang. She picked it up.

"Hi, I knew you were there. I felt it about an hour ago, right?"

"Wrong. I just got here. Must be a telepathic typo."

"Your voice sounds kind of weird."

"I have a cold. I'm nervous about going on the radio."

"Oh, right, radio. That's today. Hey, you'll be great. You know what I love about radio? The way it glows inside. Bugs like it, too. Once in San Diego I had cockroaches living in my radio —"

"Ugh. Hope."

"Really. I was in the hospital for two weeks and — never mind, I just wanted to say hi. I knew you were there. I'll call you later to see how it went."

She turned on the radio, flipped the dial: "enter into a contract"/"house ended"/"partly sunny"/"before heading for China." Every day people heard the shards of a hundred songs and announcers' voices. To go back before the invention of radio, she thought, would be to be hit with a staggering wholeness. There was a time when wholeness wasn't extinct, just as silence wasn't extinct. Now, as some writer had put it, there was a national fear that silence would break out somewhere.

She squatted in front of the bookcase, an odd assortment of art books and miscellaneous volumes left behind, she knew, by some of the various men who had lived with Hope. She pulled out *A Course in Radio Fundamentals,* a small book almost hidden behind *The Handbook of Dried Arrangements.* She tried to remember what her father had said about his early crystal set. She was supposed to be thinking about poetry. She should call him right now and ask him. Quickly.

The reason for the avalanche breakdown is found in the minority carriers that constitute the leakage current.

There had been avalanches a mile away during the rains, mud-slides the size of football fields, houses crushed into pickup sticks, redwoods torn from the earth so that their giant pulpy roots were exposed. She didn't understand the next passage either:

> Avalanche breakdown will cause the destruction of a diode if not controlled. However, with suitable control by the external circuit it can be turned to advantage since the voltage across the diode will be substantially constant over a wide range of

consent," she misread, then corrected herself:

> current.

The Poetry Brothers would not care about diodes unless a diode was an ode to the dying. She looked out the window. The man had disappeared into the motel office. He looked too shabby to be staying at a motel; he probably worked there, cleaning up.

> The voltage at which avalanche occurs depends on the doping. Light doping . . . increases it, heavy doping decreases it.

She shut the book. Her lover had been stoned, that had been the real reason, never explained. She imagined him with a joint glowing between his lips. He smoked too much, he admitted. "I'm practically addicted," he'd said shortly after they met, as they strolled near the ocean. On that walk, he had told her that he wasn't fond of water, never swam, it would put out his Aries fire. Later that month he said, "I wish I were a fish," and she said, "I thought you didn't like water," and he said, "I would if I were a fish." His contradictions, even the comic ones, made her relation to him totally conditional. "He keeps you on your toes to keep you off his back," Hope said. It was true, and he liked to keep her in the dark, had left her in the dark listening to the radio while the water teemed down her windows and her house grew as cold as if it were made of stone.

He had no radio and would not be listening to her on the Poetry Brothers show. He never listened. Sometimes he would ask her a question like, "Do you imagine my face when we make love in the dark?" but he did not listen to the answer, and most of the time he didn't ask questions. Sometimes, instead of listening he'd cut in with a song, often the blues because the blues deal with trouble and he could feel he was in trouble for not listening. "Rain hard!" he'd sing. "Rain flour and lard, and a big hog head! In my backyard!" Her father had met him once, in New York, briefly. "Kind of jumpy," he'd said later, meaning a mild disapproval that she could take or leave. She had thought they might talk about being twins, have something in common; but her father had been put off by her lover's veneer, and her lover had subtly shrugged her father off as a loser. Her father always listened, as her lover never did, but of course he was her father and his love was unconditional and undemanding. On her visit in September his eyes had watered as she stepped on the bus that would take her to the plane, her long journey away from him, maybe the last one.

Even before her father gave her her own, her most delectable journeys had been into the radio, a world that kept her company whether she was listening or not. The radio greeted her with its friendly voice on Saturday mornings, *Cream of wheat is so good to eat you can eat it every day.* Then there was the piano lesson, the radio turned off, the keyboard as long as a ship, her hands full of effort; no one had told her it could be easy. If she missed her lesson she got to hear *Grand Central Station, crossroads of a thousand private lives.* While she listened to the radio her mother was feeding her baby brother, her father was in the basement carving her a wooden boat. Where had the boat gone? Maybe *Land of the Lost,* a program where everything got found, a gold-plated bracelet, a doll's silk sock, all found soon after being mislaid, before they acquired an orphan's shabbiness. On *Land of the*

Lost, fish glided out of crevices (she imagined) and swam among watches, buttons, mittens, glided through the green shadows and the golden light of late afternoon, after-school aboriginal domain. One time she sat so perfectly still while listening to the radio that her leg fell asleep, and she stamped her foot like Rumpelstiltskin to make sure she still had feeling in her leg, that she hadn't come down with something awful, polio.

She put the middle finger of each hand on the inner crook of the opposite elbow and pressed firmly on the points that balanced excessive reminiscence. The phone rang.

"Hi, it's you, right?"

"Yeah, I forgot to water the orchid, and I won't be home tonight. Would you mind?"

"No, I like water. It'll soothe me."

"Soothe yourself. Take a bath if you want."

"No time. The program is in an hour." I'm getting frightened about my father, she wanted to say. "My throat feels raw and I haven't the faintest idea of what I'm going to say."

"Ask everyone questions. Be the Question Woman, like, remember the Answer Man?"

"Questions. Like?"

"Like, I don't know, how was your day. Everyone wants someone to say to them, 'How was your day?' But I'm not sure that water signs should go on the radio at all."

"I'm not a water sign."

"Because if you're a Scorpio, say, and you get too close to radio, it's like a radio falling into the bathtub when you're taking a bath."

"You're stoned."

"Surely, I'm at Greg's." She thought she heard a little flat-lipped wheeze, intake of cannabis. Both Hope and her lover, who hadn't called during the flood, were funnier when they were stoned, she had to grant them that. Hope blamed electricity, not marijuana, for her lover's defections. His liver had been electrocuted, she said, from the guitar he held over it all the time, a rock-and-roll high liver's liver. Marijuana was good for him: It calmed him down.

"I bet," Hope said. "I bet. I forget. Oh, I bet radio has healing properties if you use it right. Like think of those old crystal sets, like our fathers had, mine did anyway."

She winced involuntarily. The word *father* spread through her abdomen like a burn. "I don't think it was that kind of crystal; my father once told me about it. You tickled the quartz with a filament till you got to the sensitive part, but it didn't heal anything." She didn't say, I have a feeling that my father is really sick, I can't reach them, they're in the Adirondacks. She pressed inside the elbow of the arm that held the phone.

"I bet you could have a whole station just for healing," Hope said.

"KSIK."

"Whatever."

"The Head Cold Hour."

"Really."

"Or KBOD, massage instructions. Or KSLO, yoga and meditation. Or KBID, auctions of groaning cattle, sponsored by vegetarian restaurants —"

She thought of her mother shaking her head and saying, "The sicker he is, the more he kids around. Your father."

"Okay, Hope, I have to go. I'll get the orchid."

"I have to go. Did you just say that?"

"Hope, really."

"I have to go. Now I've said it. 'Bye."

She hung up and walked over to the window. Nothing. She tilted the water can gently into the cymbidium and watched water sink into the soil. "Think of Hawaii," she murmured to a whitish green bud on top, "don't forget your roots. Remember Maui,

Kauai, the black sand of Hawaii, volcanoes, terrifying rains, tidal waves." Then she saluted the totem pole and went out, locking the door behind her.

■

The day had turned even clearer. Except for a few ragged clouds to the south, over the rich farmland that grew lettuce, artichokes, strawberries, the sky was a bright even blue. She avoided the freeway and took the narrow road that curved next to the ocean, where a few flat-topped cypresses leaned inland, trained by the ocean winds. She parked in front of the frame house the radio station occupied, checked her watch, and headed for the beach. There was no sign of the flood on this street, so close to where the rains had shoveled the cliffs inch by inch into the sea, no sandbags or new construction, although only a mile away tons of sand had washed down the river and had heaped into a big sandbar, making a fast wave that only the best surfers were attempting, a hard wave with no seaweed to block the ride.

During the storm, the trunks of huge redwoods had barreled down the river into the ocean and afterwards spars of timber and swollen pieces of wood had covered the beach. People had come down with chain saws, sliced and hauled the wood, and taken the smaller pieces for kindling, leaving the useless flotsam and jetsam behind. She had seen dozens of bottles of vitamins from the Yerba Buena drugstore two miles away, and a strip of 300 ADMIT ONES from the amusement park, a pale green tangle she mistook at a distance for delicate strips of kelp.

Today it was so beautiful that if a tiny arm had waved for rescue from deep water no one would have believed it; no one could drown on such a day. The ocean was calmly having an afternoon tea party in the sunlight. Fishing boats with their bug antennae bobbed in the gleaming blue. Gulls, as white as if they had been flying through salt, banked and wheeled above the boats.

If the surf had an Indian name, she thought, it would be Water Losses. The name also sounded like something running in the seventh at Aqueduct. Her father, who thought of himself as a failure in life, had been a winner at the track. As a child she had always assumed that he was lucky because he was a twin, that *twin* and *win* were from one root. His winning streaks, she realized later, did not have to do with ambition or success but with telepathy, a telepathy common in identical twins. And her father had always been able to tell what time it was, to the minute, without looking at his watch, had been able to tell how much change people had in their pockets. For years she had been under the impression that all grown-ups could do this.

She would call after the show, although they would probably be at the lake, far from a phone; that always made her mother nervous, but her father said that was the point, to be far from everything, to take a rest. This winter they had even gone there at the height of the snow season. He'd thought of going cross-country skiing, he wrote to her, "but I always figure that somewhere around Ohio I'd get hungry."

She looked out at the ocean. Humor was a kind of poetry. As each wave curled you could see the green in it, a moment of turquoise, then the wave rolled and crashed and was over. She took off her sandals and walked along the firmly packed sand, close to the water. A wedge of pelicans floated steadily north. Is it a bird? Is it a plane? It's pelicans. Radio waves were migrating everywhere, all the time. Turning on the radio was like picking up a conch shell and hearing the surf in it. Her city niece had asked her, "Who turns the ocean on?" and she had answered, "The moon."

She started back to the station. She would call her father immediately after the show, though she knew they wouldn't be there. Probably nothing was wrong, his condition steady. She mustn't let herself think about it until the program was over; it was a half-hour show, and for that amount of time you could only have one story. Maybe her lover never listened because he sensed that with him she only had one story, the story of how he hadn't called during the flood, and that wasn't one he wanted to hear. "Stay in the here and now with me," he coaxed her. "I want to be in the here and now with you," she said, "but it's hard when I only see you now and then." "Comedian," he said, and to let him be right she told him her father's joke about the horse that liked to sit on fish.

Inside the frame house vases of freesia stood on polished tables, and a dozen records, red and purple, hung in the window, the afternoon light turning them into luminous jujubes. The receptionist, who was talking to a surfer with bony knees, said, "Please make yourself seated." Icecube Slim's program was on the air, and he was playing "Two Trains," the twins' tune. "One long gone and the other still going," the singer dragging his voice like a homemade broom over the words. She picked up a magazine creased open to an article on sound effects: "Then we added a choir from Korea speeded up fifty times on top of a wind recorded through a half-opened door." She read fast so that she could finish the article before the show started: Doctors and dentists always called you in just when you got to the best part. She had been called away to her tonsillectomy just as "Let's Pretend" had begun. They had wheeled her out to ether and sharp instruments right after *you can eat it every day.* There were complications and a high fever, and when her father played the piano for her, to cool her, she'd said, "Is it water?" not recognizing the sound. "No, it's piano. You play the piano, remember?" But her memory had gone temporarily, to the land of the lost. "I can't swallow water," she cried, her throat aching.

"To sweeten and enrich the mix we had a crowd of mummies yelling manna manna manna at high speed. Very difficult to capture was the sound of Egypt after the sun had set. But if you don't put in the moo you don't notice the cow." Sore throats had been a good excuse to stay home from school and listen to the radio — sometimes she invented them, let's pretend. She knew she was safe, the school bus on its way to school, once she heard Don McNeill leading the live audience around the *Breakfast Club* studio. She would get out of bed and march, too, to make sure she hadn't been struck down with polio as punishment for pretending to have a sore throat. When she was in bed, the *Z* on the Zenith radio looked like the word for sleep in comic books; when she was moving around it looked like a zag of lightning. After *The Breakfast Club*, she would listen to one program after another, switching the dial — *The Romance of Helen Trent, Our Gal Sunday, Ma Perkins,* while staring at her quilt, flower squares alternating with red squares, lunch in bed, *Lorenzo Jones, Stella Dallas, When a Girl Marries,* then all the programs she listened to on normal schooldays, *Jack Armstrong, Captain Midnight* (Ovaltine mugs), *Superman* (is it a bird is it a plane). And at ten after *Tom Mix* (code ring and decoder) the solid front door with the brass knocker would open and her father would try to hang up his coat as she attacked his legs with hugs, or on the rare sore throat days she would call out to him from the bedroom, her throat suddenly better, "Can I stay up and listen to?" whatever was on that night.

She heard bird twitters outside and saw a flock of warblers fly out of one sycamore tree and settle into another. Two elderly women were trudging by, holding hands, dressed entirely in pink. They were regulars in that neighborhood and around the mall. Sometimes they held magazines up to the sides of their faces so that they moved between bookends.

"Millie and Tillie," a voice behind her said.

She turned. Dan and Jon. "Are those really their names?"

"No," Dan said, "we're just working up our rhymes for the

poetry show. Not that anyone rhymes anymore. There must be a whole mothball fleet of rhyme out there."

"How are you?" Jon said. "Come on into the studio."

In the studio the air was perfectly regulated, a lower temperature than outside. She stifled a sneeze. Dan opened the window and let in a warm breeze. "We can leave it open. The mikes don't pick up the sound outside." She could hear the *skreel* and *chuck chuck* of birds, and the rush of an occasional car.

"You survived the flood all right?" she said. Their houses were on land above Boulder Creek, a town away from hers.

"Well," Jon said, his voice sounding clogged, he seemed to have a cold, too, there had been more illnesses since the flood, "we were okay but it was bad all around us. We saw a house slide downhill and slam right into two other houses. It was sliding and flashing with lights. And a few seconds later you wouldn't have known there was a house there. And the next day there was a house facedown in the creek. And the cows —" She'd heard about the cows, four of them caught in the white rapids of the churning creek, flailing, helpless, their owner racing along the banks, shooting, a quicker death, drifting meat.

"The mud was like lava," Dan said. "A neighbor of ours was pushed by a sea of mud a whole block and then trees crashed behind him and there was mud up to his neck in front of him —" He looked at the clock and indicated that she should get behind one of the microphones.

"What *happened?*" she whispered, but he was fiddling with the dials.

"Testing," he said, adjusting the small boom with the foam microphone close to her mouth. "Say, Hi Mom."

"Hi Mom," she breathed, "hi —" her voice cracked.

"Boy, you do have a cold. Well, it'll be okay." He motioned to another mike. They were almost twins but not quite, a year between them. They had a rock and roll interview show too, on which they had interviewed her lover. "He was wild," Dan had said to her. "He'll say anything."

"He'll say anything *twice,*" she had said. Today Dan had a loose string of leather around his neck, and from it hung a gold baseball, an ideogram carved out of jade, and a Phi Beta Kappa key. He'd turned his Princeton tie into a headband around his long blond hair. The hippie epoch was preserved in Santa Cruz, like fossils in amber.

He brought her a glass of water. "I'll ask most of the questions; Jon has a sore throat."

"Me too," she said. Jon passed her a eucalyptus-honey lozenge. A red light went on, so she didn't unwrap it.

Dan leaned into the microphone. "Folks, wherever you are today, on this perfect April day, the radios of the past are crackling like burnt paper. This is the poetry show."

What was she going to say? She had thought more about radio than about poetry. Radio was an idea whose time had come into her mind. She pressed the point for nervousness, the inner arm an inch above her wrist.

"How do you feel about rhyme?" Dan said after introducing her.

"Well, rhyme is a consecutive same-sound experience. With the coming of radio it became possible for people to have simultaneous same-sound experience: More people were listening to the same sound than at any other time in history. Rhyme left poetry just about the time radio came in." Her hand flew to her wrist. Her father would have raised his eyebrows at that one. "Too fancy for me," he would have said. "Most analogies are false." As a twin he was fussy about analogies.

"Yes," Dan said, "and there's also the fact that with recordings everything's become repeatable. More same-soundness. People are getting bugged by the repeatable, though, whether they know it or not. That's why people have started to long for the unrepeatable — I mean extinction, the bomb, judgment day."

"Everything but the final catastrophe is artificially repeatable," Jon said hoarsely. "I've got a friend who taped the whole storm, houses falling, dogs howling, trees coming down sounding like mortar shells. Even if it doesn't happen again he can make it happen again."

She shuddered, remembering the hissing rain, the rain drumming on the windows, rattling like bullets on the roof, gurgling through the downspout drains, dark rain pelting, and then the jarring silence after the storm, a silence that had roamed into new places, elevators not running, time standing still on dead electric clocks. Then after a while you could hear the deep rasp of chain saws beginning to slice and clear the logjams of fallen timber, while the Steller's jays cawed and flitted in the sunlight through spaces where redwoods had been. And on the fourth day after the flood her electric wall heaters had begun to glow, their fans spinning slowly at first and then quickly, humming with life. At almost that exact moment, he had called, all the energy flowing into her at once.

"You never know what people are hearing when it comes to sound," Dan said. "I know a piano prodigy whose parents only started giving him piano lessons when he was seven. They'd thought he wanted to be an electrician, because he liked electrical things so much. But then they realized that it was the *hum* he loved."

Jon looked at his watch. "But sound, for a poet, has to become language." He cleared his throat and she wondered if she could unwrap her lozenge quietly. "Here, I read this somewhere — a contemporary French philosopher says, 'Language has a double echo: from the place whence it came and from the place of death.' Is this something you sense when you write poetry?"

Her hand moved again to the point on her wrist. She couldn't concentrate on the "whence it came." Through the open window she could feel a change in the wind and then the sound of the ocean carried by the wind, a wash of voices, the voices of the dead. That's where all the voices lay, she thought, used up and perfect, eons of dead beings, sailors lost at sea, bones of whales whitening in the salt, ground by the tides into fine sand, in the water that washed past and future together, language that had never been, a spumy paradigm. When you held a conch shell up to your ear and heard the ocean's roar you knew it was the voices of the dead, broadcasting. Hadn't death come out of the radio in Cocteau's *Orphée*, which she had seen — an unlikely movie for them to attend together — with her father? *The birds sing with their fingers.* She shivered. He hadn't liked it much. She would call him and make him well. And now she would talk to them about the ocean and rhythm, the ocean and death, rhythm and death.

"Poetry," she said, but it was a whisper. She tried again, a small husky honk. She tried again, nothing. She opened her mouth and pointed to her throat. Dan looked at her with concern. Jon passed her a lozenge. She held up the one she already had; the wrapper had grown sticky in her hand.

"We'll take a short break, listeners," Dan said, and reached smoothly behind him for a record. Jimi Hendrix, "House Burnin' Down." Music of the dead, she thought. The women rock stars died of loneliness, the male rock stars died of excitement. Janis had been hoarse, a ruined throat. "I can't talk," she whispered. She remembered the acupressure points for laryngitis: They required two hands, one over the breast; she couldn't do it here. She had tried to teach her father the acupressure points for an ailing heart but he didn't believe in any alleviation except humor.

Dan sat down next to her and put his arm around her. "Don't worry, we can just play music. No problem."

"I feel stupid," she tried to whisper. A question about death had stunned and paralyzed her vocal cords. She thought of Hope listening to the program and wondering what was going on. The Answer Man. She took a piece of paper with the station logo on it and wrote under the KUSP: YOU PROBABLY DON'T REMEMBER THE ANSWER MAN.

"Heard of him," Dan said, as he pulled out a Talking Heads album. "Was he like The Quiz Kids?"

HE WAS ASKED QUESTIONS, she printed, LIKE, HOW HIGH WOULD A GRASSHOPPER JUMP IF IT WERE AS BIG AS A MAN?

"You want to answer questions?" Dan said. "We don't have a call-in line."

ASK THEM, she wrote. The Talking Heads were singing about letting the days go by, about water holding them down, about water flowing underground, water dissolving and water removing.

"Oh, okay. And you want them just to ponder, or to send in answers?"

POND — she wrote.

"Okay, but first I have to do an announcement." He turned down the record. "Are you uneasy when it rains? Do you know children who are feeling insecure and adults who are afraid to let go of control and express their feelings? Call Project COPE, Counseling Ordinary People in Emergencies, for the number of a flood recovery group in your area. That's COPE, 555-5672."

She held up her questions. WHAT WAS YOUR FACE BEFORE YOUR PARENTS WERE BORN? He repeated it to the listening audience. "Generations of Zen adepts have chewed their way into that one, folks." Jon came over to fill her water glass and looked down at the KUSP paper. With horror she watched the water run over the rim of the glass and onto the table. "It's *overflowing*," she whispered hoarsely, barely making a sound.

"I'll get some tissues," he said. Too much water has become terrifying to me, she thought, any water spilling beyond its boundaries.

Jon came back. "I'm sorry," he said, mopping up the small puddle in the middle of the table. "Like your own mind, the cup is overfull. You must empty it before you can know Zen. Just kidding."

She looked at the second hand racing around the wall clock and saw that they had two minutes left. She printed carefully, WOULD YOU RATHER BE SICK FOR ONE DAY OR HEALTHY FOR A WHOLE YEAR? That was one of her father's favorites. THINK ABOUT IT.

They walked her to her car and invited her to come back another time. LOVE TO, she printed on the pad she had taken with her. I'LL CONSULT HOROSCOPE TO SEE WHEN.

■

On the drive home through the redwoods, she tried to sing. If stutterers could sing without stuttering maybe laryngitics could sing without being hoarse. She tried out her voice the way she had stamped her foot to see if she had polio. WHAT WAS THE LAST THING YOU SPILLED? That would have been a good one. She turned the radio on, caught a fragment of something, then the road dipped down and mounted again. FM was fickle: The hills could swallow an aria, just like that, as you went around a curve, or turn it into the reggae hour. Everyone said ominously that the local Indians had said that people should never live in these mountains. Sacred terrain? No, she thought, poor reception. She laughed but nothing came out. Nothing came out the way you wanted it to. No soap. Radio. You get hoarse if you have kidney trouble, she had read that somewhere; that would be another water problem. It was *Don Giovanni,* early in the opera. How was that possible? Maybe she was in a time warp, time warped by the rain.

She drove slowly. She was near tears. When you couldn't talk, it made you cry because you couldn't tell your story, your father's or any other. Maybe if you stayed too long with a lover who didn't listen, you lost your voice. Ahead of her was the portion of road that had been covered by a landslide during the flood. It was clean and passable now, but deeper into the mountains the land was so badly changed that new maps would have to be made. A 700-foot ridge had disappeared overnight. Lompico Road was buried under 50 feet of mud. Alba Road was entirely gone. Soon, the season of enemy rain would be over and maybe she wouldn't be frightened of spilled water, but the shadow of the flood still filled the valley.

"You've been scared of your own shadow since the flood," her lover had complained. During the two days alone in bed in the cold, waiting for his call, she had seen the candlelight make her shadow big and jumpy, had watched her fear and worry grow on the wall. When she was ten, her father would turn off his Sunday Mozart and let her listen to *The Shadow* on the radio. *Who knows what evil lurks in the hearts of men?* She never told him it made her feel scared and blind. *The Shadow knows.*

She had told him about her fear on their visit to the Hayden Planetarium the last time she had seen him. They had escaped from the oppressive August heat into the icily air-conditioned dark, a dome pierced with brilliant points of light. Somehow in the dark all the things she couldn't say to him had become painfully vivid, all the comfort she had wanted to give about her uncle, about his own failing health. She had told him anecdotes about childhood instead. "*I* didn't know that," he said, and then his small human voice was cut across by the resonant voice that had issued from somewhere inside the dome. The show that day had been all about radio. The earth was beaming messages these days to 300,000 stars, a lacy cluster of distant listeners. The first message was two notes, made of light and dark spots that formed a picture of a human being. "Is anyone out there?" the narrator intoned at the end of the show. Then they had met her lover for coffee, and then they had gone, just she and her father, to the Thalia, to see *Orphée,* to keep cool.

Looking up at the Planetarium sky was like floating on her back in dark blue Atlantic water. Her father had tried to teach her to be comfortable in the water, thought she was and would remain an uncertain swimmer. He would float on his back, unflappable, urging her to imitate him, then he would put one hand lightly under her waist and let her feel the buoyancy of her whole body. When she took his hand away she didn't sink, but the next week she had to start over again: The fact that she had floated one Sunday didn't mean she would float the next. Even then she knew that water could change its mind.

After the movie, they went to eat Cantonese food on upper Broadway, the heat still bad at ten o'clock, men with big radios instead of conch shells held next to their ears. He shook his head: It was no longer New York as he knew it. In the thirties you could walk home at four a.m. and not have a worry. That was when he was writing for radio, the medium he'd seen invented when he was a boy. In the twenties he had had a crystal set made of wire wrapped around an oatmeal box, he and Arthur had had them. In the beginning it was just a piece of crystal and a cat's whisker, he had said. Later the newspapers printed new circuit diagrams every week and he and Arthur would take their sets apart and rebuild. "I can't believe he's gone," he said, his voice shaking.

Arthur's death had been hard on him, had seemed to drain the firmness and muscle from his body. He had shaved his mustache immediately, no longer needing that distinguishing difference; he no longer rhymed with anyone. She had stayed in New York for a week after the funeral, sitting silently with him, her mother knitting, creating a solicitous quiet. One day she had gotten him to watch television, even though he disapproved of it: Radio, not television, was the medium for the mind. She had found a deep sea feature on the educational channel, a film in which a diver descended deep into warm waters and played an underwater piano he had built to bring porpoises close enough to observe.

And a half-dozen smiling porpoises had in fact gone gracefully toward piano and diver, like salvaged Renaissance treasures gliding out of a shipwreck, in a voluntary ballet which the diver eventually joined. "Look, they're smiling for TV," she said, hoping her father would at least make a pun on porpoise, but he just nodded and sighed.

She felt something whiz by, and her foot lifted, ready to brake. Two bikers sped past on her right, a blur of bare muscled arms and black leather vests on big choppers. In the Cocteau movie a woman who was Death walked through the mirror, her hooded messengers two motorcyclists. A mirror was scary, death stepping through it, more frightening than a shadow. A mirror reversed everything as if it came from the other side; all a shadow told you was that you were blocking the light. After her first scary movie, she had looked into mirrors for two weeks to make sure that she had not, in some unwitnessed instant, turned into a monster. See your double and die, the saying went. Shadow you are. Was a twin in jeopardy, then, from the moment of birth?

The bikers were far in the distance now. Nothing was coming over the radio but static. She often put up with static in the mountains on the chance that some music would come through. When she told her lover how angry and disappointed she was that he hadn't called, his first words were, "Sweet baby, I knew you were on high ground." His phone had been out, the cables for that part of town had been in the bridge that collapsed over the river, but he could have walked ten blocks and called her. He would never send her roses in a long white box, never do an extra thing, never be at the exact center of her life. It was partly that she loved the slang of his fingers on her naked back and had put up with the static because of that, and partly she knew, that when you had a father who was good to you it was hard to remember to defend yourself against a man. "I thought he'd be more Oedipal," her lover had said, "because clearly you like him so much. I

guess he was a little Oedipal, but he wasn't a poor sport about it."
About her lover she knew that her father could have said much
more than "jumpy."

She heard applause, then static, then applause again; they
sounded almost the same. Classical music was over for the day; it
was rationed in Santa Cruz, like water in the desert. She felt that
everything was rationed, it had been a day of fragments. Nothing
was whole if no one was listening. She needed a totem pole to
stack up the separate pieces, her father, the water, the gulls bob-
bing, her throat aching. She passed the totem pole that stood in
front of the redwood burl store on Highway 9 — imitation
Haida — beaver, eagle, crow, woman in long wooden tears, and
on top of that a face she didn't recognize that looked like the face
of death. What did that philosopher mean by "whence it came"?
What was her face before her father was born? Her father would
have a quip for the *koan,* and it wouldn't take him twenty years.

She pulled into the garage as The Doors began "Riders on the
Storm"; she heard the phone ringing at the same time. When she
got inside the house the phone gave a tiny flick of a ring and then
stopped. Maybe it had been her lover, but she doubted it. She
knew it was time to end their story. He was, he'd said it himself,
fine for the good times but uneasy with travail. Now that the
ground was changing under everything, now that the town had
gotten serious because of the flood, it would be easier to leave
him. She hadn't felt the same about him since the flood; of
course she hadn't felt the same about him before.

She went out to the front of the house where a brick walk
curved among azaleas and rhododendrons. The towhee unrav-
eled his pleading "Drink your tea, drink your tea." A tall fox-
glove — source of digitalis, medicine for the heart — bowed
heavily; one long row of white blossoms nearly touched the
ground. A single dark red rose had opened since the morning.
The year before, her mother had confided to her that her father

had said in his sleep — twins tended to talk in their sleep, she knew that now — had said, "Roses in a cough box," and then corrected himself, "coffin box," and had awakened coughing, water on his heart. She worried that his death would make no sense to him, that it would be an awkward, sidelong death because there had been too much joking. What humor leaves in the hearts of men only the shadow knows.

Maybe he didn't want to have a death story, and what right did she have to say he should? Maybe postponement was his story, not the story of the final moment, maybe he was the dark horse looking lost at first and then coming in a length ahead of the favorite. His humor was a form of procrastination and procrastinating was a fear of change, a longing for something to be the same as it always was. But once you were dead you had a story, like it or not. Death was both the ending and the beginning of every story. Dark messengers in black leather jackets. There were angelic messengers too, winged radiances emanating from the divine mirror, but that was a heaven too rich for his blood, a heaven rich and vigilant as the planetarium dome. Angels have no sense of humor, he would have said, because they don't know the difference between the dead and the living. Why wasn't she flying home, a quick visit just to see how he was? She wanted to call but she couldn't be heard.

She would go in and make some slippery elm tea, maybe that would bring her voice back. While the water boiled, she could do some acupressure. Then she would water the garden and run a bath. She went into the kitchen, poured out the leftover water in the kettle, and turned the faucet on over the whistling hole in the top. She turned the faucet handle all the way to the left but nothing came out except a cough. She went in to try the bathroom sink. Nothing. The shutoff notice. She was sure she had sent the water company a check, but things sometimes got lost in the mail. "Land of the lost," she said, and this time there was a thin whisper. Then the phone rang and she cursed hoarsely, racing into the bedroom to snatch up the receiver.

Her mother's voice was small and worn; she imagined her calling from some gas station in the Adirondacks, or from a hospital pay phone weak from overuse and bad news.

"Hello?" her mother said. "Hello? Is anyone there?" It was a bad connection. Static, as if someone were throwing clods of dirt into the phone. Think of *yelling,* she thought.

"Why are you near a phone?" she managed to say, her voice like a weak radio signal. Her throat hurt terribly.

"I told your father I'd written to you, and he insisted you would be worried. He just wanted me to call and reassure you. He would have called but you know how he hates the phone. Do you have a cold?"

"I'm fine. Laryngitis." The breath melted out of her. When everyone in your life was alive you didn't know what high ground you were standing on. He was preparing her for low ground later by reassuring her now. He was saying, "Not yet, nothing doing, no soap."

"Tell him I'm fine. No rain. But the floods have brought out every wildflower in the book. Some five-toed geckos too. You remember those, from Jack Benny; they ate people's shadows. Oh, and I was on the radio today —." Her voice hoarsened. She lowered it like a dipstick into oil, testing its reserves. "Should I fly out there?" she croaked.

"No, why don't you just call on the weekend? We'll be back in the city."

She could see her mother's sweet worried face, like a bouquet of tiny flowers. Maybe she had been wrong to go so far from home and family, but it was natural, you moved on and you superseded: Television had replaced radio and radio, innocent as a cat's whisker, had killed off vaudeville. She would call on the weekend, coast-to-coast. People said that the rings came closer together in New York than they did in California — probably because if you were in California you had to have time to run in from the deck or the pool. Her father had said to her when she left New York, quoting Fred Allen, "California's a good place to be — if you're an orange." She always defended California but it still felt strange to her, like a map she could never refold properly, a map she wanted to fold carefully so that leisure and catastrophe wouldn't touch each other.

"I'd better get off now," her mother said. "I'm at the general store." She pictured the general store to herself, rows of dusty cans on the shelves, vegetables that could be cooked without adding water; all you had to do was heat them gently in a saucepan. In the background alert canoeists paddled through a chain of lakes that went on forever in diminishing perspective. She placed the receiver in its cradle, went into the bathroom, and tried the faucet again. It coughed out nothing. She looked into the mirror. In certain cultures looking into a mirror or water was considered dangerous. And after death you had to turn the mirrors to the wall so that the unburied dead would not reach for you. Whereas on television you had to smile.

She shivered. She had forgotten to tell him about the pianos again, for the tenth time. The ruined and happy pianos, as easy as porpoises in the water. She had gone to the civic center two days after the flood because she had been scheduled to give a poetry reading there. The door was locked, and she peered through a window into the basement recreation room. No chairs were set up. Instead two glistening Steinways, baby grands, floated in six feet of water, their bodies gliding together as if touched by an invisible tide; then they hit with a clack and slowly floated apart again. Together, apart. Together, apart. The image would have tickled her father.

The phone rang. It was her mother again. "All these dimes and quarters! Your father says he wants you to know that geckos were Allen, not Benny."

She laughed. Allen and Benny had been competitors. You had to keep these things straight.

"And he said you can add this to your coincidence-of-the-month club: He was just writing out that gecko material for Abe Stein. They're doing a radio show about the old comedians. He works so hard at everything. He'll send you the other jokes — he said there may be some you don't know."

What jokes wouldn't she know by now? Stein and Way went out to sea on a boat? There were two brothers, Together and Apart? Did this telepathy mean they would keep talking right into the afterlife, the way deep sea divers communicate with their boats? Maybe jokes bobbed to the surface even though water, which was supposed to hold you up, could hold you down. The water had collected around her father's heart as if he were the victim of a flood. *For we must needs die, and are as water spilt on the ground, which cannot be gathered up again.* That was the Book of Samuel, II, her father's name.

Where would his story end? He would want to tell her the punch line but then it would be too late to ask him, is death terrible, is it good? He would tell her that death is a horse that sits on fish. She could see him right now, saying, if death is a chicken crossing the road, what will be on the other side? So she said to the bus driver, Can you tell me when my father gets to the end of the valley of the shadow of death? But he said no.

Still Life with Bath

S HE RAN THE BATH full force into the long old-fashioned tub and then she climbed in and lay like a stone in the water, listening to the slow buoyant voice singing *You can get it if you really want,* announcing the beginning of the reggae hour. She lay tidily under the foam as if she were a stone grown tiny after centuries of polishing at the bottom of a lake. She had been taking two and three baths a day because, she joked to herself, when she took showers she thought she heard the phone ringing. They used up a great deal of time, the baths, but life was made up of time, mostly, what else was there? She slid in deeper, almost supine, sinking into the heat and fragrance, the water touching her every place up to her neck. She closed her eyes and heard the bubbles crackling next to her ears like a light distant rain. In the bath she was safe, alone with him.

They could do nothing wrong because they were inappropriate from the start; every move they made, in any direction, brought them closer to the end. There was no waiting to understand what time had in mind for them; it had nothing in mind, though it would let them dance. They spent hours flying to each other (watching time go backward or pull forward), New York, California, New Mexico, New Hampshire, substituting enormities of space for the skimpiness of their future. He traveled to play music, she traveled to give lectures, and the rest of the time they lived 3,000 miles apart, talking on the white phone that was now perfectly, whitely, silent. He might be anywhere.

"Where did we see that crazy guy wearing the sandwich board that said I NEED A WOMAN?" he said. "Was that in Soho? On Telegraph Avenue?"

"The streets were really dirty."

"It wasn't L.A."

"No, it was cold."

". . . that week in Santa Fe when it snowed, no, there are so many women there. Can you imagine having to advertise?"

Sometimes the exact tone of his voice would come back to pierce her before she could attach it to meaning, so that it went directly into her body. Adver-*tease*? His musical voice would say it in an upward, querying tone, marveling at everything. He loved to talk, loved to hear her talk — "Come on, what do *you* think?" — loved all responsiveness in speech, comebacks, repartée, compliments given and taken, ensemble work. He was the only distinctly handsome man she had ever met who didn't secretly want to be alone.

"I just called to hear your voice," he would say after she picked up the white phone. "Say anything. I get this literal physical feeling when I talk to you . . ." And he would listen to her as if she were music, the sound waves from her body corresponding to some perfect score in his mind, just as their bodies fit together perfectly in gesture — dancing, sleeping, making love, standing close together on a crowded train. "Listening can be difficult," he said. "Most things don't make a sound. The carpet, for instance, is silent, but everything can be touched, everything can be seen." She liked that and wrote it down, everything can be touched, everything can be seen.

She stretched her head out of the bath like a tortoise without losing the touch of the water around her shoulders. The small silver clock she had set on the floor would tell her to get out before her fingers began to wrinkle and whiten. She reached for the soap, remembered that she was clean, and lay back with her eyes closed, letting her cupped hands float like paws on top of the water.

He had told her about his childhood. She saw a blond boy with slate blue eyes and a face as luminous and defined as a caroler's on Christmas Eve reading in a room in Yarmouth Port, his mother considerate but rarely smiling, never wearing a pretty summery dress (as *she* was as he told her this, he said, his hand distractedly lifting the lace at the hem), his window facing the nine-foot tide: "You could walk all the way out and it was only up to your ankles." He was flanked by silver and gold trophies (track and soccer), by the Martin he now played for a living, and by his father, who leaned over the dinner table, lobster faced, furious, so constricted by opinions he had trouble breathing in the violence of getting them out. Once, with her, he had dreamed it, his father's voice pounding him awake, his blue pajama top shamed with sweat.

"But you're so luminous," she said. "You were bright and good, you must have been loved." She didn't say that he was like an aspen lit from inside, smooth white bark in October light. Tiny leaves spin green and open and breathe and drop gold.

"What about you, your parents?"

"I'm older, it doesn't matter."

"Sure it matters."

"Well, my father disparaged her down to her bones. It made her crazy, finally, certifiably. I got out early and saved myself." He held her immediately, sensitive as fast film taking in light. He stroked her hair, soothing her as if it had just happened, as if she were not calm. It shocked her to realize that without telling him he envisioned her mother plucking at the muslin curtains and making pottery at Morningside, sliding off in the long, silenced ambulance. She had put things away and now he was taking them out again, carefully, as if he were handling quail eggs, gently commenting on the flecks darkly mottling the shell. His cogent kindness broke her heart open in one clean gesture and she suddenly felt she could not live without him.

He had already fallen in love with her, quickly, like a snap judgment that had the depths of years of consideration. He insisted that it was not enough to be loved as she was already loved by the man she was seeing, you had to be loved for the right reasons. "You're gentle, you're witty, you have a sense of honor," he said. "I've been searching for years."

"You haven't been alive for 'years,'" she teased.

He ignored her; he was in pursuit, persuasive. "You're a Jane Austen heroine with the body of a sassy — the way your waist goes in, here, your breasts —" He showed her, turning her to face the full-length mirror in the light of the one candle, opening her thin robe, giving her her image with his hands on her, as if he were softly rubbing his vision into her skin. She closed her eyes and felt his ten fingers as twenty fingers, telling her the story of her life — she had never heard it before.

"I used to think nineteenth-century heroines didn't have bodies," he said later as they lay in the wide bed, his own body palomino, a thin film of perspiration on his chest, a faint silvery smell on his skin. She watched his chest rising and falling, watched the curtains glide inward in the evening breeze, stirring the scent of jasmine into the room. They talked till sunrise.

"When I was ten I was worried," she chattered. "I thought I'd never find a boy as smart as I was to kiss. So I let Billy Emerson come over, he was very good-looking, and I tutored him. I told him, '98 percent of the people in Colombia are peasant farmers.' When Mrs. Penniman called on him in class he said, '98 percent of the people in Colombia are pleasant foreigners.' I couldn't kiss him."

He laughed. "I would have liked you at ten. Such a serious girl. Of course when you were ten I wasn't born yet." She thought of their reflections in movie lobby mirrors, of the occasional sharp glances from passersby, women his age the worst, clear-eyed and condescending. Once they had cataloged those glances, in the beginning, when it was almost amusing: Boston's were meanest, San Francisco next; New York and Los Angeles were indulgent and saw them, holding hands, as young lovers. On a bus from Worcester to Lee, where friends had lent them a house in the Berkshires for ten days, a house filled with American antiques that would burnish their impermanence with continuity, they relinquished themselves to the plush seats, relieved to be setting out on a journey together, and heard Yankee voices behind them.

"How you doin', Louis?"

"Gettin' old."

"*That's* healthy."

"Goin' to visit my kid brother."

"Jackie?"

"Yup. Gettin' married. Woman twelve years older than him."

"Aaaaiiyyeehh," the man sympathized. "Poor fellow."

"Well, you know, she's got a business. He's in it for the green."

It was the first time they had avoided anything together, sitting there without speaking, her head buried in *Anna Karenina*. Vronsky was younger, she was sure. She herself had no green, so there was no question.

■

She lay back in water tinted by pine bubble bath, sealed in by the steam and fragrance, sinking that memory in the heat. She lifted some silky foam on the back of her hand. "When I was ten I took lots of baths," she murmured into his absence. "I remember this plastic elephant that had bubble bath in it, how you squeezed it to force the liquid out the trunk, how at the end when there was none left the elephant wheezed and wouldn't come back to his shape. He was all dented and you could only get a few drops out. . . ." She imagined him laughing at the obviousness: "Sexy *girl.*"

She stretched out her leg and touched the cool knob above the faucet with her foot; the knob had metal toes around its circumference and she tried to fit her toes around them. The night before, after the routine and minor insomnias of her solitude, she had dreamed about an elephant at the San Diego Zoo, where she and he had once walked through the hummingbird house, iridescence flashing in constellations through the humid green, a metabolism like his when he played pickup soccer, winning as usual, moving fast, she watching from the opposite bank of the Charles River. The birds, emerald, vermilion, azure, some the size of minnows, dazzled him, but he worried about their freedom.

"They're gorgeous," he said, "but they can't *go* anywhere."

In the dream the elephant nodded his head while a white peacock, its fan trembling inches above the ground, spread a nuptial light through the grass and trees. The latticework of wrinkles in the elephant's skin was the sign of his long memory, like creases in the cortex. He brought up his trunk and with its sensitive tip felt for the shape and temperature of her neck. With that trunk he could pluck a delicate leaf or uproot a tree. His touch vacuumed her out of herself and sent her rushing into the white surprise of morning, where the elephant's absence was a blaring emptiness.

∎

She tucked her hair more cleanly into the yellow shower cap. She had assigned her unconscious a dream about her hands and had received the elephant. Her hands were striped with veins, "the way my mother's were when I began to pity her for her age," she thought. The ridges at her wrists made her uneasy, dry creases like the kneefolds of elephants. Time was right on top of her, changing her skin so she couldn't breathe, pulling her through a tunnel that led away from him. She saw herself at seventy, gaunt cheeks, silver hair, wrapped in a woolen shawl, returning to sheep, her next life, keeping her eye on the jump of the sheep until she was asleep under the earth or ashes over the hills. . . .

She fashioned a kneeling sheep from the foam in the tub and let it graze and tremble and collapse on the curved rim: white oval without stilts. The dream was clear: the elephant was a man: she liked men but she didn't like all of them. Her efforts to make the wrong ones interesting had worn her out. Yes, she could understand having to advertise. She knew it was wrong to think of him so much; even the reggae didn't condone it, Jimmy Cliff in limbo saying, *All that is passed and gone, this little boy is moving on.* But she preferred to bask in the half-life of their shining, sunk in that pluperfect realm where she remembered him saying, "This is golden; it's like gold pouring down, being with you; it's like light."

The music almost drowned the cat's meow, but she was alerted, she had been waiting for two days, understanding too well the force that drove him out into the night of dogs and coyotes, that kept him running, wandering, exhausted, not grooming himself. She climbed out of the tub to let him in; the coyotes had been shrilling earlier, yammering and yammering. She ran to open the sliding door, leaving islands of foam on the blue rug, and found him seated just outside the glass, the moon rising like a mango above him. Old stolid long-haired male - he padded into the kitchen for his waiting food. "His black-and-whiteness makes me want to read a book," she murmured into space, sinking gratefully into the hot water. "Oh, precious, precious," he would admonish, chucking her gently under the chin. But he had liked the things she said, even though he sometimes caught her out, as she caught him out.

The music was moving on now, up and down, sultry and dignified, *No woman no cry*. They had danced to Bob Marley and the Wailers in a ballroom on Columbus Avenue, the Wailers' hair like live twigs smeared with ocher. They had danced like wands, like waves, like semaphores, had made love like pistons that night, a real screwing. Bob Marley was singing about anger and hunger and how connected they are. That was politics of course but if you wanted someone and you couldn't have them that too made you furious. She remembered the insinuating sound of the drum played by Peter the smart boy she chased in high school, one light conga so exquisitely timed it hurt, two notes the same and one down, the sound of a dent being made, off, somehow, not where you expect anything to happen. She liked things off, unstable syntax, the frothy white ballerina pirouetting among the syncopated dancers in red Hawaiian shirts shrugging and swaying to the Beach Boys on a stage where overalled dancers sprayed graffiti on a backdrop that rolled upward, allowing them more and more clean canvas, another chance and another.

And after that dance concert, the night before one of her planes to California, they had gone back to the Seventy-ninth Street brownstone he was taking care of and they'd played pool. She'd watched him right-angled over the table, his rump up, that perfect curve, the bright clack of billiard balls on green felt under the chandelier, his grace and muscle teaching her how all the balls would fit eventually into the pockets. He hadn't liked the ballerina, a solecism. He liked Mozart, tennis courts, geometry of ebony circles on white soccer balls, everything perfect. Having set up his absolutes, however, he liked to improvise, and before going to bed they played hockey with a broom and bagel down the long Italian-tiled hall, the bagel banging up against the cream-colored walls, she bent over laughing, ("C'mon, Raggedy Ann, *play*") and when he won by inches — "Goal!" — he took off her clothes.

∎

She pushed the door closed with her foot to keep the heat in, the reggae lyrics buried now in the impeccable, staggered rhythms. *Go get your weakness and dance. . . . keep lion up yourself. . . . ah so far. . . . sapphire. . . . so vi-cious. . . . so se-rious. . . .* she couldn't quite make it out. There was no literal truth anyway: He had said they would never lose sight of one another. She remembered the exact words, spoken at the end of one of their marathon conversations on the new phone, with its dry, respectful, erotic ring, the white phone that allowed him to get through to her anytime. They had talked three hours, four hours, five hours once, sickened by the stale intimacy of the plastic receiver, unconsummated by touch or sight — he was wrong, not everything could be touched or seen — but unable to hang up. He had made love to her over the phone: "I want you." They were murmuring into the receivers, inciting each other, when they heard voices, a mother and daughter in Santa Fe and Wisconsin, a conversation about herbs, midwestern, innocent: "You should always collect the leaves in the morning after the dew is off, then just spread them out on the floor to dry."

"You're on our line!" they cried out, inflamed, as if a shade had snapped up and their neighbors now peered in at them writhing in joy and abandon on a rumpled bed.

She was really alone with him now, in that limbo where her mind, sometimes in a loud whisper, worked out the figures of her longing against a wallpaper of silence. She had become accustomed to soliloquy, loneliness, the single voice, a solitude that worked so deeply on her it seemed to alter her fingerprints. His actual presence had kept her from echoes; after being with him she always felt at one with herself, smoothed into shape. She breathed more easily then, as if inhaling a meadow's sweetness, fragrance of cowslip, oxbreath, self-heal. Often he played the guitar and sang her to sleep in a rich tenor-baritone that was clear at the center with the slightest roughness at the edges, like tiny cilia that picked up feeling from the air. When he sang to her she became a child, time slid over so that he had more of it, sleep releasing her face into a youthfulness he remarked on. He sang piercing, primitive, Irish songs, Beatles songs, the blues, and his own songs whose abruptly modulated melodies seemed to come from a place where things existed in their original condition, without anger, without irony, without pain. He and she were as intimate then, as he sat on the bed coupling them in his harmonies, as when they were making love.

She put the hot washcloth over her face to avert the memory. She remembered that when someone asked Einstein how he found his theory of relativity he answered that he found it because he was so strongly convinced of the harmony of the universe. She had cried when she read that; she wanted to cry now about something that had nothing to do with her. But her mind whispered to him behind her back, I need you, there's nothing here, the world turning blue only when it moves into darkness, soft and bearable then, your blue eyes gave me more sky, your gentleman's face, your cheeks, your really nice mouth, the Renaissance curve of your eyelid, lashes and hair on your arms a true gold in the sun, a joy inside me you always meet —. She began to cry, a wrenching, coughing crying that felt ammoniac in her sinuses, ungainly, awkward, a ten-year-old's heartbreak. She pressed the wet washcloth to her tears. I want I want.

The cat pushed open the bathroom door, tiny live oak leaves nestled in the fur of his tail like jewels. Did the cat remember that strong hand plowing through his fur, joshing, a male hand, "Hey, Pico, how you doing? Hey, Pico Boulevard. Pico della Mirandola.

You have black, you have white." She took the cloth from her face. The reggae was louder now, a slow rhythm, a rhythm that sank to its knees before it got up again. Then Earl Zero was saying, "It's a rough life, but after a while you see the benefits, later." His voice reminded her of deep blue smoke, distant coffee plantations. "I and I paralyze all weak heart conceptions," Zero said. I and I, that curious plural. They had not made it to plural. "We're a hybrid," he muttered to her one night when he had fallen into a scrabbling darkness. "Nature hates us."

Unhappiness transformed him as she had never seen anyone transformed by it. "*You're* the one who's luminous," he said, "I'm just flashy." His blond hair would darken considerably in his misery; she didn't know the chemistry of this but she saw it happen. A vein would bulge in his temple, faint imperfections in his skin would show up as pits in his complexion. He would leave the light on then, all night, to guard his fragile sleep, and get up in the morning blinking out the new day, his eyes as sensitive as an albino's. "A headache — I have them often — as if I hit my head on a drawer."

Sometimes he would go back to sleep and she would wait an hour or two, pretending they had plenty of time, the shadows lengthening as if in the dour interior of a Flemish painting, lengthening until he woke up again, when he was sometimes silent until dinnertime as she moved in an eager hush, ready to speak or silence herself if it would help. His play of shadow and light drew her in and the return of his light was always worth waiting for; it felt like a morning light, all objects fresh under its gaze.

"What do you do to have fun?" he said. It hadn't occurred to her — a blurred category. Books? Walks in the woods? Travel with the man she'd been seeing? He took her to the arcade at the amusement park and chased her through the constantly changing maze, the shrill electronic beeper announcing it to everyone, then she chased him, the silenced beeper telling everyone he was hers. They were a perfect match, each wanting the other in the white labyrinth on the black screen, each determined in pursuit, each skittish in escape. Then they played the pinball machines, the most garish one, FUTURE SPA, he expertly releasing the ball so it made contact — there! there! again there! The hits lit up for him, SPA! a hairsbreadth between no touch and the touch that won everything. The ball dropped down in the gutters and raced back up again teasingly near the FUTURE zone when a good-looking girl at the next machine gave him a long low-waves Hawaii satin look and he lit up — he looked at all pretty women as if they were the highest waterfall in the world, with a delight and amazement that no one could mind — and lost interest, the ball rolling down to the bottom making no contact, disappearing, a clear miss, darkness, you lost your chance.

They sighed and moved on to the machines near the door of the arcade where the late sunlight streamed in and presented all the gold in his hair. While he was jabbing at the controls of LUNAR RESCUE she put a nickel in the YOUR MATE machine that sat mutely in the midst of the ululations, menacing roars, twitters, beeps, gurgles, sick lost plane noises and groundbreaking explosions that flashed around her in an atmosphere of continuous emergency. The card it dropped for him had a blonde on it, circa 1932 she guessed, before even she was born. Across the way FREE PLAY winked like a pulse above his head, rewarding the quickness of his hand and eye; he was at home in those electronic complications. The card was musty and ancient. Your mate. The girl was dimpled, with ringlets, plump in a gingham dress. A matching blonde. Adorable as a kitchen window. They would have three children and live in an ivy-covered cottage with roses lining the walk. He was in luck because she would make the most perfect wife. A picket fence. He thanked her politely and looked away.

It was dusk and they walked near the ocean, the sky a mulled blue, an hour when the day asked nothing and gave nothing, the colors so easy "it feels like we're floating in water," she said. They were alone on the beach, the sands crisscrossed with cracked wood, dank with kelp, detritus from the rains. The sun had gone, the air still warm, with a damp coolness brushed into the center. He kissed her a long time and she could feel his tensile strength, energy coursing through him almost visibly, as if he were at his best in a waning light. They walked on, holding hands, and he turned to her, barely able to see her expression.

"I'll want children, you know, in seven or eight years, when the music stuff dies down. I don't know, maybe I'll go to law school, write music at night. I don't want to be a performer all my life. I really would like kids, three kids, even, I have to be honest."

His warning stunned her. She had not thought that far ahead, had always left mathematics for last, even in high school. These numbers made it impossible. "We'll keep it light," she said in a thin voice pitched as carefully as a tent against the weakness scattering through her.

"You know, it's not that I have a taste for older women, I don't, in fact. It's just that I love you. It's awful, unfortunate. But time is part of who you are."

They made their way back to the boardwalk, an electric fairyland with the lights of the roller coaster and Ferris wheel behind. She shook out her pride — she hadn't needed it with him before this — and let it billow around her into his accurately unconsoling silence. They gobbled corn dogs, drank terribly sweet root beer, hovered over a tower of cotton candy as if it were a pet or a child, taking turns licking the bands of sticky pink until they reached the bald paper cone beneath.

"Awful stuff."

"I know, but it wouldn't be . . . *amusing* . . . without. . . ."

"Yeah."

She let her body ripple and let go in the fun mirrors, lengthening into giraffe as he telescoped into midget: She was grateful for aberrations that had nothing to do with age. He poised a rifle on his shoulder three times and won her an animal — "That one!" — a huge stuffed dog the color of cotton candy, with a button nose and a mouth that puckered downward like someone speaking French. She carried it next to her face so she could feel the plush against her cheek.

"I wish summer could go on and on," she said.

"Autumn will be cooler."

They ambled back and forth until the crowds thinned out, the screams and the noise of the roller coaster's heavy wooden machinery all around them. They wanted to walk off the conversation, exhaust themselves so they couldn't remember it, although he would never ease out of it and say he hadn't meant it. "Please never get between me and the truth," she had said when they first met, sensing an honest man, someone she could ask that of. He had understood her exactly.

Now it was late. "Hey, Big Time?"

"Yeah, Big Time?"

He put his arm around her. "You look tired."

"Never tell a woman my age she looks tired." She moved away. Just one hit of bitterness, she promised herself, and then she wouldn't do it again. He was being straight, after all.

"That doesn't sound like you."

"It isn't me, it's some old lady," she said. Two hits, that was the limit.

Their lovemaking that night took place in a realm so deeply fitted inside time's mysteries, so close to the peak of time, that it released them wholly into themselves. Time being divided, she had read somewhere, was only another bad idea of someone forcing strife upon unwitting souls. The only benefit of divided time, that she could see, was that it led to music. He was minutely attentive and then fast and furious as if he were racing the twelve years between them, making up to her as hard as he could the insoluble gap.

"You look like a waif," he said afterward. "God, you look sixteen." He rocked her whole long body to him. "I'm sorry. I love you." Because she was older and knew how time flew and memory failed she kept a journal for the two years she was with him; later when she reread, "I'm sorry, I love you," she tried to reconstruct the seconds in that pause, to remember whether there had been a pause at all. Of course there had been.

The only way to forget that she loved him was to forget him entirely and she could not do that; it would be a dishonor and a defense. She held to an absurd fidelity that she feared would be literal, and worried that with another man she would mistakenly cry out his name because it had the status of an animal sound for her, the tearing call of a coyote or a leopard's growl, inextricable from pleasure at the moment it had lost itself in that brilliant sirening blankness just before collapse. Memory was integrity, and if she were to be exempt from it on account of extreme pain there was something even worse — at some point the pain of remembering would become the pain of forgetting: his face would elude her, the taste of his body, the faint scar on his hand from soccer, the curve of his shoulder that her mind sculpted over and over, his skin simultaneously rough and smooth like velvet rubbed in the wrong direction.

The cat unfolded and repositioned himself into an oval next to the tub. The cat always stayed close when she thought about his body, as if she gave off a warmth, a pulsation, delectable hues. The cat must see it in her as clearly as she could see the moon. Once as they lay nude in the living room on the carpet among the semitropical plants, moving as slowly as cliffs shifting on the earth's surface, the cat had come loping in from two rooms away, eager to be a voluptuary, too, licking and biting their hair, rubbing against the giant faces that must seem like bodies to him.

They had made love in every room of the house and, if she allowed it, every view out every window released a memory of him. She remembered them in the kitchen, the scent of roses in a glass fractured as she forgot to breathe as in the middle of cooking his ham and eggs (she was eating a persimmon, satiny orange pulp smeared on her lips and chin) he reached an arm out to fold her to him, very deliberately switching off the gas jet without looking behind him, wrapping his hard muscular body around her, so that she felt not only loved but claimed, lifted out of some desolate abandonment she hadn't known she existed in. In the translation they were always making — love with a plus or minus twelve in it — intensity was their only permanence. Her legs turned to water and she let him, she remembered thinking of it that way at the time, do whatever he wanted with her, a streamer flashing across her brain: "I'd give up anything for this."

That was the period of the names, when he made up lovely names for her every day, like someone bringing flowers, until he decided on the one that was best for her. He also had a niece of the lovely names, he told her. His eyes turned slightly bluer when he talked about her. He did like children. "She has this wonderful way of talking," he said, "Like a bird singing in its sleep."

They were listening to subdued Mozart, music for glass harmonica, in a restaurant on the water. He looked at her across a table set with blue napkins, cornflowers, gleaming crystal. "If we had a child she'd be so smart. . . ."

"She?"

"And have coppery green eyes like yours —"

"And soft lion hair like yours —"

Then they both looked pained, as if someone had pinched their faces with a metal clip, and he began to talk about his own childhood instead. There was a time, he rushed on, the summer he was seven, when his family was at the cabin in the Maine woods and after dinner they played Mozart on an old record player (sometimes she said record player and he corrected her, "Stereo"), the first time he'd really noticed music, by a composer who seemed to understand counterpoint and harmony since babyhood, his mother told him, a child no older than he was.

"I would have been nineteen," she thought, "working in an office to earn my way through college, while he sat very small in a green wicker chair, up way past his bedtime, listening to the Sinfonia Concertante against a bath of cricket sound, listening to the life move in it, completely at home in his own small life."

He was sitting there, he said, fighting sleepiness, when a buck, antlers young and wide, and then a doe, and then a fawn on fragile legs, emerged from the forest in the silken moonlight, holding perfectly still, completely at peace, elegantly gathered in the light to listen, ears flicked erect. "In a way it was my first experience of quietness," he said. "You have the kind of gentleness they had. And, you know, that evening made me understand in some dim way that music brings things to you. It made me think that if I could play music an elegant peace would come to me." He laughed. "I'm still waiting." He reached for her hand across the table, ignoring the waitress who splashed ice water into their glasses. "Well, *you've* come to me, anyway."

"Am I an elegant piece?" She laughed.

He didn't mind her lightening it up. She was just drawing back as she did sometimes when he held her so tight she felt like balsa, breakable, the way he drew back sometimes, too, each of them fully responsible for this walk along a precipice. They would distract each other as if they were invalids with months to live, playing gin rummy at midnight, baking apple pie at two a.m., watching Katharine Hepburn on television till dawn, giving each other little quizzes ("What two plays are about moonlight?"), reading foolish comic books when they were most anguished; "Could this be Paradise?" he intoned, "Or is it only temporary before a real terror besieges them? Bound by pure love they share a secret knowledge of a mythical garden. And fate has smiled on their union, for few people who enter the twilight zone are ever allowed to return."

She pushed up a little in the tub and felt the refreshment of the air on her arms and shoulders; its sculpted coolness had a more knowing touch than the warmth of the water. She let one hand dangle over the edge of the tub as if her wrist were broken, her other hand weaving the air in time to the music, *get up, stand up.* She could hear the lyrics more clearly with her shoulders out of the water, but the air had a disturbing smoothness and she slipped down again into the bath, into the beginning.

The dream had signaled that she was going to fall. They had made love for the first time and she was astonished at his perfect body, a Leonardo drawing of man accepting himself, justly, humanly, loving himself. She opened easily to him and to the luxury of trust: He was too young to hurt her, he could be a real friend. They laughed, wrestled each other off the bed, read aloud to each other, smoked joints, ate chocolate cookies, and walked blindly on a moonless path he knew by heart. His laugh was sexual, a full wet brushstroke. Applied to paper it would be the blue of the Pacific on a glittering day, surfers out in the high clean waves.

She had fallen asleep immediately in the narrow bed. The dream signaled that she was going to fall. Buildings around a grassy court of classical proportion. Pitch black and no sense of space as she knew it. The ground gave way and she was taken into a dark unending fold of earth. From her throat a shout that coated itself in fear and became a whisper. The falling renewed itself even after the thud that woke her and sent her, shaking, to the sink for a glass of water where she found a leaden colored mouse floating in the basin like a bloated rag. She had known what the dream meant and had flouted the omen. He was like sunlight; it would be worth it.

■

She heard the click of acorns dropping from the live oak trees onto the porch. The water was cooling now, the reggae sulking and cajoling, doling out measures of insouciance, then silence, the singer withholding his favors. She waited, swished the cooling water, then he began again. She turned the faucet to hot and brushed the scalding water into the cool. The Jamaican dialect was difficult; it sounded as if he were talking about weather, talking about weather as if weather were sex. His rich voice hoarded all the meaning in the world; anyone who wanted it would have to go to him to get it. She shut off the water and heard the announcer reel off a list of titles: ". . . and 'Telephone Bill Too Big,'" he concluded. She was sure she'd heard it right this time. Their telephone bills had been enormous.

But the radio and the water had stopped helping. His absence was audible now, a sound only a dog, maybe a cat, could hear, a sound that shifted atoms so that the room looked different, odd, her face in the mirror odd. His looking at her face had become part of her face: "It's a pretty face, a serious face, sometimes not so pretty, always interesting, beautiful." It was now dimming to nothing, non sequitur, a place to carry her eyes, a face going no place. It would drive her crazy to think of him so much but the dullness of not thinking about him would take her strength from her.

Only one more and she would stop. It was July in their second year, their last night together, they had agreed on it. They had seventeen hours left, plenty of time. The night was so warm, the two-lane road so smooth and deserted, the moon so bright, that he turned the headlights off and let the car glide into the middle of the road, the yellow line spinning out from under them like a spider's thread. He held her hand tightly in the middle of the seat as she tried to memorize the comforts of their silence.

"A dog!" he said, his reflexes quick, his foot on the brake, his arm flung out to keep her from pitching forward. She saw a small brown dog, flaggy tail flaring up behind, running quite fast and then, as her eyes adjusted, the shoulders of two men — what were they doing in the middle of the highway? — and then the shoulders of the men, she saw, were not the shoulders of men but the rumps of horses, two white horses trotting, a dusty white in the warm dark of the evening. He slowed down to a crawl and the dog earnestly herded the horses to the left side of the road till they were alongside the car and she could hear the clop clop clop of their hooves over the sound of the motor.

"I can't believe this," he chortled.

"Horses. Horses!" she cried. She could not get enough of them. Their dusky whiteness was evenly paced with the car, their wildness moving heavily through the silence, their secret animal strength close to her, powerful bodies that made the metal of a car seem ridiculous. They glided alongside in the shadows made by trees and moonlight.

"We better call the police."

"The next house."

They drove on and passed no houses but within a minute saw two pinpoint lights enlarging as a pickup truck came toward them out of the other end of the night. He put the lights on and flicked them fast, afraid that if he slammed at the horn it would frighten the horses, who were moving ahead now, the dog, harried as a man wringing his hands, trying to stop them. The truck slowed as it came alongside.

"It's a good thing you're a careful driver" — the man at the wheel leaned out — "I thought we'd lost them altogether. Keep going, we'll follow," he instructed them, and the pickup swung around in a U-turn.

The horses were going faster now and cantered down a side road that branched off to the left. Then they began galloping in the silence, their rumps dusky moons, the dog keeping up, the surrounding mountains patient, moonlit, still. They swerved at a farmhouse with a barn behind and disappeared into a meadow that sloped up into orchards. The pickup bucked to a halt.

"Is this your barn?" she said.

"No," the driver said ruefully, "thanks anyway," and he and his partner hurried toward the meadow with ropes slung over their shoulders. She felt small, disappointed, as if some rushing stream had stopped. What she really wanted was to run with the horses, run into the night.

"I didn't really want them to catch those horses," he said.

"Me neither," she said, though when he said it, it made her uneasy. "They were beautiful."

"Incredibly beautiful," he murmured. "They looked exactly alike."

■

She turned the faucet to the left and waited to feel the comfort of the hot water replenishing itself. Of course he wanted babies, flesh to bind him to time so he wouldn't get lost in it, someone to look exactly like him. The water ran lukewarm and she absent-mindedly soaped her breasts and shoulders, the foam in flat white islands around her. Linton Kwesi Johnson sang with alluring menace, *I did warn you,* concluding the hour, as the water ran cooler. She squeaked the knob to the right and got out, dripping, to stop the plastic pulse of disco, he had hated that jabbing continuum.

She crawled sopping wet under the sheet and blankets, something she'd learned, you healed as your body dried in its own good time. Once, tired of California, looking for differences that would mask the real difference, he'd said, "Healing, why talk about healing, healing implies you're sick." The bathwater gurgled down the metal drain into the earth, an odd tintinnabulation, like a phone ringing. She stared at the white phone in its hospital silence. Inside, it was empty; there was a dark anonymous knowing buzz. Perhaps she had only to pick it up and he would be there, in Boston, Los Angeles, Santa Fe, telling her he loved her, wanted her, right now: That was craziness.

Someday, probably, he would call, make the dead phone jump, and she would say, "Fine, fine!" but she didn't want that cartoon of cheerful conventional pride, she wanted the close-grained things all over again, the old precincts replayed, with new lighting to diminish the lines in her face and erase the twelve. She pulled her knees up against her chest under the covers and pulled her head under, to increase the heat. She had to stick to memory and the simplest things. Time would not heal her, it was not on her side. She shivered a little and thought, "Even my hair gets lonely," and she left the light on as a memorial as she settled down to sleep.

Falling

LAURA PULLED AWAKE, breathing hard, but the dream was gone. Crystals at the window flung rainbows onto the wall; little fish of light swam searching for a stable place. The day was going to be hot. She dragged the blanket up to her chin, hearing his voice, as cool as wine, saying, "Do you really need all those covers?"

For a minute she dozed, then boiled awake. The space for his clock radio startled her again. Her clock was round, everything there on its open face. On his digital clock one moment had tapped the next on the shoulder and told it to get lost, the used up minutes dropping into oblivion, disposable, like the music he woke to, music like Styrofoam. He could use it, he said, his serious music fed on what was in the air. Laura wanted the rock and roll they had listened to in Los Angeles in the seventies, when everyone was happy, when they cruised the freeways between Porsches and shiny trucks, listening to music so rhythmic it could keep you in your lane even if you forgot to steer.

A rapid knocking on the wall made her sit up. For weeks the woodpeckers had awakened her, pecking holes in her sleep. Every night she put earplugs in, the way the woodpeckers tucked acorns under the shingles of her house, but then she heard her heartbeats as if they were someone's footsteps coming to find her. *Get out of your nightgown.* A sock she hadn't noticed clinging to the flannel crackled as she peeled it off. He was supposed to have called the day before, about shipping the piano to New York. He was always late, he thought time was his, was only where he was.

In the mirror her eyes looked shallow, the eyes of an animal hit by a car. *Soon you'll start looking old, then you'll always be in a bad mood.* The clothes in her closet seemed dead. She knew she dressed sanely every day, though how she couldn't remember. Pride was like fat — everyone had it in a different place. At least there were no moths flying out of her dresses this year. She washed her face, opened a compact, and absentmindedly dusted rouge onto the small mirror. *Not again.* This week she had stopped for a stop sign in her rearview mirror, a stop sign on a side road a block behind her.

■

The cat sat on the other side of the bedroom door, his black paws drawn in, his posture courteous, his meowing importunate. "I'm up now," she said to him. "Now what do I do?" He trotted ahead of her to the kitchen, throwing a look over his shoulder, as if to suggest a gourmet breakfast. She was too tired to know what to eat these days. Since Nick had left, her sleep had been full of dark and sudden drops. At four in the morning she would panic awake as if falling from a trapeze. "I'm halfway between wheel-chair and trapeze," she had told her divorced women's group, and they had nodded sympathetically. She could go back to bed and satisfy herself, fitful fantasies drifting into relief, but there was no point, it was worse than nothing. *Get moving.* She had been making two cups of coffee every morning since she had asked Nick to leave, homeopathy against bitterness. In California people did not like to hear anything bad. She had told no one that on one day she couldn't remember how the receiver was connected to the body of the phone, on another she couldn't remember how steering wheels were attached to cars.

She shut her eyes and tried to visualize the refrigerator handle a few feet away from her: Was it vertical or horizontal? She could picture a refrigerator, but it was the run-down one in the house in New Hampshire the first summer of their marriage, humming with the secret privileges of vacation houses. She saw herself reaching for the handle in order to get the lemonade she made every afternoon while he composed. He sat loose-limbed at an old Baldwin working out the song cycle he later dedicated to her, based on the colors of her voice, he said. She pruned the image of him until it was perfect, the lamplight a halo around his face and shoulders. Her voice had disappeared after their first couple of years together, although before they were married she could sing for hours into her solitude, lost in the drowsy confections by Fauré and the faceted jewels by Mozart she knew by heart. After he'd left she had tried her voice out with the radio, the last live Metropolitan Opera broadcast of the season, but it was a badly caulked voice that could hold no breath, energy leaking out of it like wind under a door. She reached for his COMPOSER cup and her spine shivered: A small moth drifted out of the cabinet, colorless, its languid flutter eerily unresponsive to light. The moths had come last summer, folding themselves into her clothes, floating out of the closet with a leisure that showed they had the upper hand, a constellation of confirmed suspicions. Now she would find them creeping through the rice and flour, secret as ash. There were smears of silver powder all over the sides of the cabinet where she had crushed them. She had dreamed of them shudderingly, not as themselves but as a single rat covered with baked cheese, browned and bubbled, poking his nose into a saucepan on a rear burner. Mothballs were toxic; she had had her quota of poisons.

She shook out a vitamin B tablet, poured a cup of coffee, and went into the living room. The cat sat watching the ficus, digesting his ancient boredom. Her houseplants, like canaries in a mine, would let her know if she were in danger of dying. In the dream someone had been letting the cat out of the bag, blowing the cat out of the bag. No, something about wind, air pressures clashing, high and low. She took out the atlas and blew a film of dust from its edge. The atlas was a ghost atlas, full of outdated borders and countries oblivious to the liberations and usurpations that were yet to come. In grade school the pale maps pulled down over the blackboard had always made her sleepy, as if they were shades pulled down for the night. She propped her unemployment form on the map of Africa and checked off the appropriate boxes. *Did you work in that week? Did you try to find work for yourself that week?* Now that she was alone she had to answer to anyone, her buffer gone. *Did you have a change of address that week?* No. She pressed harder on the Congo. Why must everything change? There were good reasons.

∎

If he had been there he would have put on music by now. In the past year it had been his own music most of the time. He had gone from writing for instruments — silver, ebony, spruce, mahogany, brass, pressed directly by hands and mouths — to composing with synthesizers, pieces committed to endless repetitions, morose and unedifying. His new music had made her jumpy, had made all his previous work seem innocent as sunlight. After a while you find sunlight boring, he had said, as his trips away from California increased, concerts and lectures swallowing him up. She had continued with her teaching job at the university until her contract was up, had made do with the redwoods and windy beaches, attached to pleasures she no longer enjoyed. She had saved enough for a year, for getting her bearings, if she could bear them.

The craziest she had been was in the three days after Nick had left, three months ago. She had listened to the Four Tops singing "Seven Rooms of Gloom" a dozen times and calculated four times seven equals twenty-eight times twelve and so what; she, divided by him, was nothing. Now she lost things, unpaid bills, sweaters, ballpoint pens. They eluded her, whereas he had been a finder; things jumped into his hand, eager to be near someone who had math and music in him, who would not be unnerved by an x or a y. She had lived on cottage cheese and tequila and soundless TV for three days, then she had abandoned the tequila and allowed the TV to fill her mornings, afternoons, evenings, letting a machine keep her alive.

The refrigerator changed gears and she went in to look at it. Another summer, later, they had been in Shaker country, a yellow farmhouse at an intersection of green hills and peaceful roads where everything was joined to the thing before and the thing after. The Shakers were careful in their shaking, they shook in a stable world. They had invented the flat broom, the washing machine, could sew invisible seams in linen and wool. The light in those hills had been so clear and sharp it could have taken photographs all by itself.

A year ago she had asked Nick to take some pictures of her. He was an expert photographer, at home in a confident medium, but that day the only frames he didn't blur were the frames in which he chopped off her head, leaving a close-up of her full breasts in her Roy's Market T-shirt. He had always been bothered by that edge in her face where character interfered with prettiness. No one liked to be reminded of thought or conscience in the middle of making love, especially if he was a liar.

As his lies had multiplied, her amnesia had increased. Now her memory was slipping away so quickly that when she remembered the past it felt only slightly familiar, like a premonition of the future. "I have seen the future," she said to the cat, "and it's the past. Don't worry, though. In California here to there is more important than then to now. Memory isn't essential, but you really have to have a car."

She knew the amnesia was protecting her, too, from recent shocks, the flash flood arguments, the gasp of his suitcase zippers as he packed to leave. Some loss of memory was natural, a shedding, but caterpillars and all liminal things must intuit the next stage, their molting like fresh clothing, not like sacrifice. While Nick lived with her there would always be more of everything, but now that he was gone none of it would happen again. And if he lied and if she had no memory, she would have no history, and if you had no history, time became heavy, like a machine that runs all day and manufactures nothing. Like television. Most mornings she sat there absorbing the game shows as if they were sunlight, waiting for *All My Children*.

"Soap operas are realer than novels," she said to the cat. "They go on and on." He chewed mental cud, mulched her words, emanated consolation. "On television nothing lasts more than a second; you can hardly remember what remembering *is*. And color TV is using up all the color in the world. People barely notice that for the past twenty-five years everything around them has been fading. Things have been going faster, too, but of course you've noticed that, haven't you noticed?"

Eat something. She'd had only brown rice yesterday and the day before. When she opened the refrigerator and lifted a block of tofu out of the greenish water, the tofu crumbled into three pieces and fell on the floor. *You lost him: butterfingers.* She took out a bag of Pepperidge Farm cookies and tore open the package, leafing through the nutrition magazine she'd left on the counter. In California food was the site of big conversations: I was sick but now am well. *When plants are exposed to stress they emit poisons.* She opened the closet where she kept cookbooks, earthquake supplies, onions and potatoes. The smallest potato, veiled with green, looked sick. She poured out some Crystal Springs: There were unacceptable traces of everything in the local drinking water. *Some pesticides, when combined with others, are fifty times more toxic than when used alone.* Could the hints for healing keep up with the catastrophes? *After she had eliminated tomatoes from her diet her pain was entirely gone and she beamed with gratitude and joy.*

She had never seen so many doctors. She would talk to the divorcées' group about what it felt like to go to a doctor when you no longer have a husband, someone who has been inside your body 3,000 times. You needed to go to a doctor because you needed someone to tell you you were all right. Maybe she was going to be touched. In order to be touched.

She disliked being part of the flight pattern of divorced women. She objected to them referring to themselves as survivors. True, they were learning to live without love, money, safety, grace. But there had been no holocaust, they had not been tortured or blasted with radiation or left for dead. They were not even like Scarlett eating radishes at Tara, everything burned down around her. And all of them seemed to be resentfully, permanently, celibate. But how, without sex, could you get to the wisdom on the other side of the world?

■

The cat sat with determination at the sliding glass door. She let him out, then followed him onto the deck. When she looked at the garden she could not keep herself from counting — six yellow roses, four red, three dusty pink equals thirteen, unlucky? Beyond the garden lay the Zayante fault, a small quarry studded with madrone and lined with shallow caves where children played in the afternoons. It was his fault, though they would get a no-fault divorce. There were more divorces in fault-crossed California than anywhere. Couples who had gotten along in Nevada would suddenly start to quarrel on the other side of the state line. They would be stopped for fruit inspection, they would see the luminous orange disks marking the lanes of the freeways and feel the terrifying lightness of the air, and then they would begin to fight.

And although the personal cracks and fissures might be there to defuse the big ones you still couldn't count on things staying in place in time. What did that do to your sense of place? I don't belong anywhere. Where am I? She was all loose in wonderland, alluvial valley's liquefaction potential, sandy, unstable soil. *If I eat bread my fingers turn black,* the magazine said. Eve was tempted, and ate, and the ground shifted as she awoke out of Eden into time, aware of the heavy wind that was Adam's breath bowing across her throat. When your roots are gone, everything moves. By the year 2000 California would be a mass of scar tissue.

Laura aimed her face at the sky, her mind jumping. She knew she shouldn't be lying out on the deck like that, the ozone shield torn away. What did you do when your source of energy turned against you? hide? compromise? give up and die? The cat walked over with his mature gait, so old now he ignored the tiny lizards darting back and forth on the heat of the wooden boards. He lay down in the chaise in the cool shadow made by her body. He had come to their door eleven years ago, one night when they were cooking fish in the cottage in the Hollywood Hills and feeling happier than she could remember. Now he was too old to recapture the territories he had lost to the younger toms. They had argued about getting him fixed and then stopped arguing. Slowness won most of their arguments, Nick's slowness, especially: Fighting with him was like walking through sand dunes in a dream. His *ritardando,* a friend of theirs had said, was different from hers; his was to make people wait, whereas hers was to let people catch up.

She felt for the cat, sunk in an elderly purr, and leaned over to pet him, trying to keep her hand relaxed so that her touch would feel kind. The first thing a pianist learned was how to relax the hands, Nick said. But his hands had changed on her body after his mind had begun to wander; his hands were like wind that made her jumpy. She should go in and jump on the trampoline for twenty minutes. She could play music as loud as she wanted; during the day her neighbors worked at Monolithic Memories in Silicon Valley. They had heard only the arguments that took place in the evening. It was better to live here even if you worked there: Helicopters had been spraying the other side of the mountains with pesticides for the past three weeks but they wouldn't do it over open streams and a thick canopy of redwoods. In such a fragile ecology people were friendly to their neighbors. But after ten years of consent she was weary of California people: Conversation with them was like constantly having to be polite in front of paintings on velvet.

The hushed roar of the wind in the pines sounded like a kettle full of water just before it begins to scream. Laura lifted her face to the sun; it would heal the small wound on her brow that had scabbed over once and opened again. She fingered the rough spot and saw that her fingertip was streaked with red. In what opera was there a wound that didn't heal, a symbolic wound? She liked the quizzes that came on during the intermissions of the live Met broadcasts. Nick had taken her to dozens of operas before he had stopped liking opera. Mozart, Puccini, Verdi, all replaced now. Evenings in red satin and thrift store rhinestones, Nick handsome in a dark suit, their feelings moved huge distances by the music.

She sat up. The hummingbird was dipping its bill deep into the red-hot poker again, bleaching it of its red nectar from the bottom up. The *chip* sound after it sipped was like children's scissors going *snip snip*. The tiny berries on the rosemary hedge were a dusty blue. A hawk hovered over the arroyo; in his placid eye his prey was already jelly. The matilija poppies — white crinolines

with gold knobs at their centers — dropped against their props
and strings. Someone would have to tie them up: Put it on the
list. She was sure that if you went long enough without sex you
forgot the names of flowers. She almost had it: There had been
wind in the dream, not a nice wind. The sun slid out and reached
for her face and she let it hold her, hungry for the feeling of im-
mortality a suntan brings.

■

The valley was already an oven, the heat like a curfew maintain-
ing quiet. Over the narrow highway that led to town the redwood
trees cast their long-legged gloom. She did not look at the
scenery now; to do that you had to be in the passenger seat. In
front of her was a black Chevrolet pickup truck with six letters
painted out so that it said CHE. Steve liked to talk about politics
but she didn't feel up to it today. She had known him since she
was in college and he was in law school. He had given her a lift to
New York at Thanksgiving and in the settling November dark
had described his childhood in hiding in the south of France. He
had told her about the sympathetic concierge, the Christian family in the country, how he was hidden under potatoes in a wheel-
barrow, someone moving him out of new danger into a safe
place at the monastery. His father had been shot in the back. His
mother, an opera singer, had died shortly after she got to the
camp but had not escaped being forced to sing with the concentration camp orchestra.

Now Steve was a lawyer in Cambridge, visiting California to
interview victims of industrial sickness in Silicon Valley and to
see a young cousin in Santa Cruz. In their few visits together
Nick had pretended Steve was a rival, even though he thought
him only dull and decent, because there was only one kind of intimacy Nick understood. She had never taken that seriously but
now there was a wisp of hope in her.

The redwoods led her into town, to the LEFT ONLY painted yellow on the highway, past Henfling's, the redneck bar, and Eats of Eden, the health food store, which faced each other across the main street, evidence of the uneasy truce between the old lumberjack locals and the Haight-Ashbury émigrés of the sixties. She parked behind a green Ford pickup with a German shepherd in the back. The dog snarled at her, pressing against the barrier. Concentration camp dogs; now everyone had them. As she crossed the street she heard the driver say, "Shake it, baby," and she walked faster. She couldn't quite believe that in a minute she would be protected by Steve's familiar decency and seriousness, here in these mountains. She wondered if he would think it odd that she hadn't invited him to her house. Whenever she could, these days, she ate in restaurants because they made sequence so clear: You ordered, you waited, you ate, you paid, then it was over, as if one gesture were fastened to the next, as if something were really happening.

As she entered the cafe she heard the first notes of "I Fall to Pieces," Patsy Cline. The cafe's air-conditioning seemed to be broken. The chintz curtains, the poinsettia, looked tackier in the heat. At the back was a large poster that said CHOKING. Steve was already there and he rose to hug her, the first time she had been touched in three months. She was surprised by her embarrassment. He looked different. He wasn't wearing his glasses, his eyes soft and dark behind contact lenses. Confronted with his angular serious looks, his new gaze, she felt like confetti.

"How are you? You look a little shaky."

"I'm okay, it's just hot."

"It's all fog downtown. I took the bus and hiked a river trail and it was fairly cool, but it's suffocating up here." He'd been perspiring, dark circles at the armpits of his blue oxford shirt. She looked at the lovely stretch and curve of his chest. His voice sounded deeper now that he wasn't wearing glasses. He had always had a rich mahogany voice, the ghost of a European accent, reliable and agreeable.

Even so, she couldn't hear him very well. Lately people's voices seeped back into them as they spoke rather than coming toward her. Nick had developed a hearing problem in the last months, really a listening problem. She had had to repeat herself. He of all people knew how things became either ridiculous or sublime through repetition, how you could make fools of people just by forcing them to repeat themselves.

"How's your cousin?" she asked.

"He's a Buddhist now. Marketing meditation. He's got a big Victorian at the ocean with the guy who owns that vegetarian pizza place. Yesterday they were doing kundalini headstands and watching *Star Trek* reruns at the same time. He thinks everyone's lost and the only way to get yourself back is to buy yourself back."

"And we always believed that you don't sell out in the first place."

"Heard from Nick?"

"He's in New York, on the verge of being famous." She didn't want to talk about it, not yet. She forced herself to notice the menu, its delicate calligraphy like alfalfa sprouts. A flyer on the wall advertised workshops called Have You Lived Before? and I *Do* Deserve It. The small business cards taped to the cash register would be for shiatsu, carpentry, horses for sale, lessons in channeling music with the help of higher forces and the redwoods. She had lived here a long time.

"Laura, are you okay? When I saw you last year you looked like you were going to get a divorce the way a woman looks like she's going to have a baby."

"I couldn't trust him anymore."

"I always thought you had an arrangement."

"It was a bad arrangement. And on top of that he rearranged it."

He smiled wryly. "Who can trust anyone completely? Not that you didn't do right."

"What's trust if it's not complete?" she said.

"Laura, in California you can't even trust that the ground won't give way under your feet." He patted her cold hand. She wanted to grab his hand, hold it a long time.

The waitress appeared and he took his hand away. She wore a T-shirt that said:

COME CLOSER

and in smaller letters below that:

not that close

"Sautéed tofu with veggies, scrambled tofu with whole wheat toast — we better watch out or we'll get health food nerves," Steve joked to the waitress. She looked at him blankly. Easterners always did this, forgetting California's allergy to wit. The earnest visitors swished this shallowness around in their minds, thinking it had a depth that would be revealed by further exposure to California sunlight. The waitress, blonde and pale, looked as if she had been reconstituted from a powder, pastel, no aftertaste. Laura wondered if the phone number on the menu — YIN-YANG — was new, she had never noticed it before.

"There's a best way to trust everyone," Steve said. "You just have to find the right way. Are you anxious about the future?"

"I'm anxious about the future because I'm losing my memory," Laura said.

"Of course you're losing your memory, you're living in a place that doesn't have any history"

"No, it's me. I can't remember anything." She felt as if she were

confessing to a drinking problem. Everything seemed too heavy
to lift to speech.

"But tell me how *you* are," she said, after they had ordered.

"I'm very good. Seeing someone new. Very new. That is, very
young and very recent." He pushed the bridge of his nose as if he
expected to find his glasses there. "Melanie's a teacher. I went to
her class to lecture on the Holocaust. I've been doing this in pub-
lic schools, a program called Never Forget. The kids ask questions like, did the Jews wear gold stars because they were good,
did you see Hitler, if you had a number on your arm would you
wear long sleeves after the war? I've had all sorts of memories —
my mother singing Brahms and Schubert to me —"

She had seen someone with a number on her arm, months
ago, where had it been? No, she'd just had her hand stamped with
a blue saxophone at the jazz club, that was all. No, now she remembered. A short woman in her sixties on the stationary bike
on her right at the spa, pedaling hard, breathing hard. She had
disappeared before Laura could talk to her. Laura had been busy
talking to Willow, on her other side, Willow who had given her a
few messages, read her Tarot cards, who was tall and blonde, a
gentle California beauty. Willow sewed tiny crystals into the seams
of her leotard so she could take on heavier Nautilus weights. Minor
magic could move you around when no big wind had blown you
into the mouth of history. Laura felt split apart as she panted on
her bike: On her right was a woman who had fallen through the
huge crack of Auschwitz or Dachau or Birkenau and had landed
in wonderland; on her left was Willow, pedaling gracefully, her
casual tranquillity so distant from the specifics of the sequence of
numbers on the woman's arm. The numbers sewed the woman
into her place in time, irrevocably, while Willow floated above
hers, playing with consciousness, with the body.

Steve was looking out the window, his eyes large, soft-focused.
Laura stared at the digital stutter of his watch, minutes that led to

nothing. In the new physics, Nick had explained to her, time and space were just a bunch of chopped up seconds and atoms. If this fact fell into your heart, she thought, you would die of it.

Steve seemed unable to bring his gaze back to her and she followed it to a figure in a long white dress moving lightly, like snowfall in a paperweight, toward the cafe. The woman wore a white turban and an amethyst pendant that flashed back at the sun. Willow. Willow had announced three months before that she was leaving for Las Vegas to sing with a band. Laura remembered Willow's gentle hands spreading eucalyptus oil over her back and felt a retroactive gratitude. Then the screen door wheezed, a warm breeze floated into the hot cafe, and Willow sat down. She put her hand over Laura's, the second time Laura had been touched in an hour. Sanity was a matter of knowing whom you're allowed to touch.

Willow flashed a blonde smile at Steve and Laura introduced them.

"Laura, I dreamed about you last night. Some kind of wind."

Laura felt a *frisson* scissor down her spine. It made her want to take a nap.

"I can't believe this heat. Do you suppose I have skin cancer?"

Willow leaned closer to show Laura a scaly patch at the juncture of cheek and nostril. Laura smelled honeysuckle, rain, something not quite so sweet. Why hadn't Willow asked if she could sit down?

"All this skin cancer means sun worship is finished. Forget Apollo. We have to return to loving the moon, our mother. Cancer is our national punishment for not believing in the invisible." Willow's diction was clear as water. "People are using their third eyes to watch television."

Laura looked at Steve, expecting raised eyebrows, but his eyes were relaxed and consenting, the pupils large. In her white dress and turban Willow looked alluringly lunar. Laura felt a triangle forming, felt a metallic edge around her body and a prickling in her hands, like when strange dogs barked at her.

"I was a sun goddess in the first grade," she said without thinking, in a voice without energy. She had wanted to be cast as the normal girl matched with the normal boy in the play but she had been given the biggest part because she had the best memory, had been chosen for a singular role, with a yellow muslin dress and a wand encrusted in crunchy glitter. What was the chemistry of self-pity and what could you eat to change it?

The waitress set down their food. "There you go."

Willow ordered eggs and toast and mint tea and turned to Steve. "You're about to take a trip," she said. She closed her eyes, opened them again — lupine on alpine slopes. "To Yosemite. For — a week?"

Steve ran his hand roughly over his hair as if he were thinking in a courtroom. "How could you know that?"

Willow smiled. "I'm psychic if I like people. Everyone in my family is. It's our way of being polite."

Steve let out an amazed laugh. "I'm going to camp above timberline with my cousin. At a place he says there's no trail to."

Laura could see a hundred miles on every side, air thin and clear, water trickling through the cracks in boulders. *Take me.*

"Are you going, too, Laura?"

No, Laura thought, looking into Willow's blue eyes, noticing how dark her lashes were, *we are not a couple. Read my mind. And I'm afraid of high places.* She felt a twitch in her upper lip, as if water were trickling down it.

"I'm not afraid of heights," Willow said. Laura jumped; she had not spoken aloud. "Once I was, but I cured myself by teaching myself to fly in my dreams."

The waitress set down Willow's food. "Oh, I got a muffin instead because the toaster's broken," Willow said.

"No, it isn't broken, the cook is just doing muffins today."

The waitress came back a minute later. "Do you have ESP?"

"I'm just good with small appliances," Willow said. With a small movement she lifted off her turban and bent her head over her plate. Steve stared at the silky curtain of hair falling on either side of her face.

"We borrow our necessary densities from the plant and animal kingdoms," she said, looking up, "but we rarely say thanks. I wore this turban a lot in Las Vegas because of the trip with men. Men and women aren't opposite in the right ways anymore. Especially in Nevada. Anyway, it's all jackrabbits and mesquite out there. And Thor wanted me back, when he got done leading the treks in Yosemite. And the band disbanded."

Laura wondered if Steve would be afraid of lightning and thunder above timberline. Long ago he had been quietly terrified of the thunder cracks that reminded him of the bombings during the war. He had told her that, basically, there were two kinds of people, the ones who are afraid of falling from high places and the ones who are afraid of things falling on them, and the latter were always those who had been through a war. He hadn't thought about California, where people were afraid of falling into new cracks in the earth, gaps born out of a quaking thousands of feet down.

The table shook for ten seconds.

"Subway?" Steve laughed. Laura scanned the room to see if there was a table big enough for the three of them to hide under.

"There've been a lot of tremors lately," Willow said, "but we won't have a big one soon. Cats and dogs aren't running away, the way they do before an earthquake. Thor always checks the classifieds for missing pets." Steve looked impressed.

Laura said, "I read somewhere" — she wondered where — "that to an animal there is no such thing as Los Angeles."

"There *is* no such thing as Los Angeles," Willow said seriously. "Places all over are losing their auras. Most places are nowhere and we feel it, but they're still on the map so we get confused. The way food has no nutrients anymore."

Like Nick's music, Laura thought.

"I was sorry to hear about you and Nick," Willow said. Laura knew that the amethyst crystal hanging over Willow's heart was meant to magnify compassion. Willow put her hand on Laura's. "Not all bad things are harmful. And you *are* strong — people must have told you that."

"No one has told me anything," Laura said. Nick never had.

Buildings could have fallen down inside him and she wouldn't have known. Yet by his silences she had been molded, told what to do. Willow's searching eyes looked at her sympathetically. Nick had thought Willow was beautiful, had flirted with her the one time they met. Willow, on a somnambulist's plane that day, had seemed not to notice. It was during a stretch of time when Laura felt that he hated her, had finally told him that. He had flatly denied it, looking bored with the idea. "Don't *lie* to me about *hate*," she had shouted, rushing toward him, raking four tracks of blood onto his wrist. He had grabbed her, held her hands so that they blossomed from his grip like flowers.

"What will I tell people?" he said later, and she said, "Tell them you were attacked by a rosebush."

She excused herself and headed for the bathrooms marked THEM and US, next to the CHOKING poster. She chose THEM and leaned over the sink, splashing her face with cold water. Their anger had not been the clearing anger that brings a second chance. In this small space she could hear his pacing, a pacing he, in his repressed fury at her, would extend beyond his study, as if she were not sitting in the living room reading, or standing in the kitchen cooking dinner. A certain number of measures one way, then the same the other way, then back again.

One day when she came back early from the store she thought he had extended his pacing to the garden, but then she saw that he was leaning against the fence, talking into the cordless phone that had nine memories. He was murmuring, but her listening was so refined and urgent that she could hear him through the screen door, her hands pressing against the doorjamb, her head down, as if she were praying her way through an earthquake.

"I will *certainly* call you," he said in a voice full of tenderness. A spot on the top of her head burned. He was supposed to tell her if there was anyone; that was their arrangement. They would rebuild their Eden out of honesty, even if other people snaked through their lives. She was sure the woman on the phone had something to do with the sharp changes in his music recently. When he had played his first electronic piece for her, a piece in which he undermined memory by eliminating melody, she had said of the withholdings and repetitions whose incessantness pressed her against a wall, had blurted out in her first disobedience as a muse, "Isn't this just a case of the emperor's clothes?" And he had responded without missing a beat, "In California the emperor doesn't need any clothes," and walked out of the room.

His pacing, then, had grown slower and slower, a torpor of self-regard, the distinction between movement and immobility harder and harder to define. There was a drag in his voice now, a drawl scrolled with confidence. He didn't want his music to provide the feeling of a beginning and an end, he said. He didn't live in human time, she thought; he lived without pain. She had had to ask him to leave, finally; all his meanness, in his own good time, would have taken the stuffing out of her.

She ran the water again and patted its coolness onto the back of her neck. A week after the murmuring he was back in New York again. He called one morning at nine his time, six hers. "Sorry, I forgot," he said. He needed a phone number from his revolving file. She stumbled sleepily into his studio but couldn't find the file anywhere on his desk.

"Try the top drawer," he said, when she came back to the phone.

In front of the file in the drawer was a stack of snapshots, the top one a double exposure of three people. She recognized Lincoln Center, the stony plaza. Winter light brought his handsomeness to full pitch and definition. Whoever had held the camera had inspired his happy boast in the lens. Laura had not been to Lincoln Center in four years; yet she saw her own bony sculpted face, with brown hair that looked like shreds of confetti, posing under a floating geranium. Plastered to her face in a double exposure was the face of a woman with electric black hair, half of the woman's features lost in Laura's, the other half unblending. Nick had taken a whole roll of Laura to make up for the blurred pictures and had unthinkingly reused the film; she had wondered where it had gone. After the argument, the day he came back — anger melting them together like records on a hot day, so annealed that no free joining could ever take place again — she had learned that the woman was a cellist, someone he had been seeing for six months, although at first he said he barely remembered her, his eyes blinking wildly. She had always thought of cellists as dowdy and sad, their legs spread for only one thing, the music, but this one wired her cello for duets with her own amplified breathing and had been on the cover of a magazine.

She rinsed her face again, avoiding the mirror, feeling stuffed with heat and sadness. She was glad Willow was there, to do the work of talking; she realized she had been depending on Willow from the minute she sat down.

They didn't look up when she returned. "This net of conceptualization, that's what's making the world sick," Willow was saying as she ate her crumbly muffin with boarding school composure.

"The world is sick because people don't think *enough*," Steve replied, their eyes locking.

Laura felt as if a piece of her back were falling away; nowhere in the world was there anything that was hers. Willow's eyes looked like flowers being fed by water, and hers must look like lumps of clay.

The waitress came with the bill. "How did you like the eggs? The cook wanted to know because the recipe came to her in a dream."

"Perfect," Willow said.

■

The waitress turned the sign in the window to CLOSED and they went out to the car. Willow would drive downtown with them, and Thor would pick her up later. Laura slid behind the wheel; it was too hot to touch and she put Kleenex under her hands. Across the street in front of Valley Discs Used and New, six records had been set out to warp and twist in the heat, local humor.

"The trunk of my car is full of earthquake supplies," Willow said.

"I keep them in the kitchen closet," Laura answered. Canned fruit salad, soup, Ak-Mak crackers, cat food, chile. She'd seen a moth glide silkily in there too, its whiteness like the blank space between her hands that didn't catch it.

Once they were driving under the redwoods it was cooler. The bumper sticker on the car ahead of her said GIVE PLACE A CHANGE. No — GIVE PEACE A CHANCE. Steve sat between the two women, close enough for Laura to smell the graininess of his sweat, his sweet, near-vanished aftershave. Up ahead a man in khaki stood next to a wooden barrier, a car stopped in front of it. Had there been an earthquake? Laura surreptitiously extended two fingers, hexing the stop sign. She knew that Steve got uneasy at borders. The man in khaki peered into the car. "Do you have any fruit?" he asked. A small insignia showed that he was with the agricultural service.

"No," Laura said. "Have they moved the state line? Are we entering Nevada?"

"They found a pregnant medfly in Boulder Creek," he said, unsmiling. "Strawberries are okay." He gave them a copy of the afternoon paper. Leaning close to Steve so that they could all read it at once, Laura thought she could smell Willow's honeysuckle scent coming through his body.

Two helicopters arrived at 10:00 a.m., circled the periphery of the nine-mile spray zone and then began to spray.

As the helicopters were first seen, residents and store owners ran into the street to watch. "This is really exciting!" said Wade Snegmer. "It's too bad they aren't spraying at night," said Lompico resident Helen Hoglen. "It's beautiful over in San Jose when the helicopters light up the sky, like fireworks."

The water district fears the valley's open streams could get a toxic level of malathion because of the dripping from trees and the runoff into streams.

The entire county is now part of the emergency area and may be sprayed up to eight times.

"But they said they wouldn't spray here," Laura said faintly. She thought of the way lies had smeared Nick's voice. He had gone, but now the lies were coming from elsewhere and fog would drip malathion into the open streams and make a toxic mist over her world. People had run out in it. Soon they would have beauty pageants for Miss Sun Damage, Miss Black Lung, Miss Acid Rain. Whereas other people would develop a dread of the future and a loathing of the past that had contaminated it.

"The earth will take care of herself," Willow said. "Reseeding and dying and reseeding. In the long view —"

"But what about *us?*" Laura interrupted. "We're selfish, we want memories, we want homes and meanings —"

"Have a nice day," the agriculture man said to them, waving them on.

When they stopped at the red light in Felton a young man came over and handed Laura a lime-colored flyer. She passed it on to Steve; it said MALATHION at the top. Willow asked to be let out. Did she know something? Laura didn't want to ask — it would be like asking a doctor or a lawyer for his services free of charge. Then she noticed Thor, who was walking into Big River Books, a woman leaning close to him.

"I have to do a property check," Willow said coolly, sliding out of the car. "I know that woman," she leaned in to say. "All her planets are in the house of death. Steve," she said, smiling. "Laura — stay safe and beautiful." She wafted across the street like a gorgeous moth.

Steve looked at his watch, as if he wanted to notice when time had stopped. If he were Nick he would have found a way to keep her there, see her again. Maybe he would.

"Unusual," he murmured, to say something.

"I thought you liked her."

"I did." He blushed and began scrutinizing the flyer.

"Tell me what it says," she said.

"Read it later," he said, folding it neatly in half and putting it in her purse.

"Well, is it more bad news?"

"It's just information. Dos and don'ts."

"Like, don't breathe?"

"No, breathe."

"How sick are those women in Silicon Valley?" She felt sorry for them.

"They're pretty sick."

"I thought so."

"You have to take the long view; things can change."

She turned south onto Graham Hill Road, climbing out of the Valley, and blue sky slowly faded to gray, the redwoods reaching up into the fog. The sore on her brow stung a little. She decided not to touch it. The somber trees whizzed past, spokes of light flashing through the branches in a strobe effect. *That can cause epilepsy. Don't look.* Who had told her that? She had no idea. Loss of memory was like fine china breaking. Sip. *Crash.* Sip. *Crash.* Was amnesia a form of clairvoyance, the memory of a foreordained extinction, soon to come? Maybe her memory was leaving her to give her a sense of possibility, as one of the women in the group had said. Laura had tried to tell her that she thought it was more serious than that, something close to real amnesia, but she had forgotten the word for it: "You know, whatever that is when you forget something."

■

At Main Beach, Laura shivered in the foggy chill. Next to the sidewalk that bordered the sand, tall trios of palm trees alternated with two-faced parking meters. A block away the latticework of the roller coaster made a backdrop to the patterned trunks of the palms. Laura had heard there were rats in the palm trees. At the Coconut Grove ballroom the CASINO sign pumped red to green to red in the bleached afternoon light. She and Nick had gone to a Halloween ball at the Coconut Grove. What had he gone as? Something false, a cape and mustache. She had been a salad, a seamless green, without dressing.

They went down the concrete steps to the beach, the calliope's music drowned out in the ocean's roar. Shorebirds skimmed the edge of the surf, almost touching the breaking waves. The fog brought out the harlequin colors of the rides and the long arcade. Willow had said that auras were easy to see near the ocean. Laura thought she sensed a whiteness around the crown of Steve's head, like white fuzz on a strawberry, moving fast. His aura was gathering mold. Out of boredom with her. Or it was a vitamin deficiency, hers.

Out at sea a thin stream of shearwaters made its way south. Nick knew all the birds, all the squashes, all the fish. She was surrounded by streaks, impressions, deliquescing puzzles of color and light and shade. Maybe the waves would bring her memory in — each wave as it lapped the shore bringing the thing she wanted to remember and depositing it on the sand.

"I'm fascinated by water," Steve said, as if it were orchids, a hobby.

"Willow told me once that singing next to bodies of water can increase your telepathic powers," Laura said, her voice sounding dry to her. "I think psychics are so big in California because it's a way of controlling the world through the mind without really thinking."

"Maybe." He shrugged. "But when you trust your own perceptions the way psychics do you worry less about trusting other people. Time holds fewer surprises," he said gently. Maybe the young Melanie had told him this. He seemed like a stranger to Laura, lighter, changed, not on her side of misery.

"It took me four years to get over the breakup with Rachel. And we weren't married as long as you were."

Laura tried to remember what Rachel looked like, a quiet person, a round face. How long ago had it been, the four of them at a party, Nick flirting in every direction, drunk, Steve's awareness of it an unintending gilding of her humiliation? Steve had hinted that Nick loved her unhappy watching because it spooned manna into his narcissus pool. She had taken his chivalric concern for granted then; it was surplus, mere friendship. Now she wanted to pay attention, but if you paid attention only after you needed people this much were you merely using them? The women's group hadn't discussed this.

They stepped over a tangle of olive-colored kelp, a cloud of gnats flying around the ridged leaves and rubbery bulbs. Insects collected near people who were angry or frightened, someone had told her. She stamped on the kelp to feel it pop, then listed into Steve's tallness and almost tripped. He didn't reach for her.

"Of course now it seems long ago," he said.

Maybe he would help her with her history over dinner, when she had the courage to talk about it. Surely he would stay for dinner after he'd made the effort to get to the mountains, after Willow had taken their time away. They would have turkey burritos in the old Mexican cafe across from the boardwalk or clam chowder on the pier where sea lions with whiskered faces lay on the rafters barking.

"You seem brave," he said. She shivered. That's what people told you when they meant *don't ask me for anything,* even if they liked you. A few feet away a lone seagull was tearing a fish apart. She could feel him thinking about leaving.

"Let's just walk as far as the pier, then I should go," he said.

She felt space widen around her as if she weren't sure where anything was coming from, as if she were constructed around an absence that would put wind in her bones. "Now?" Her voice croaked. Was he leaving because of something prearranged with Willow while she was in THEM? She wanted to drop to her stomach and hang on to the sand. *Not everyone is Nick,* she reminded herself.

Steve put his arm lightly over her shoulder. "Take care of yourself. I wish we'd had more time. But I need to talk to my cousin a bit. Maybe I can get through to him. I'll be in touch soon."

She let him hug her, the third touch of the day, and then walked quickly, blindly, in the other direction. Somewhere there was a vocabulary she hadn't learned, a vocabulary that made other people act the way you wanted them to. She did not want to go home to the poisoned valley, the malathion wafting in from Boulder Creek, moist, ammoniac, punitive. She did not want to buy food for dinner, because when you were alone the supermarket Muzak went straight to your bones, the grinding buzz of refrigerator cases, the smell of locked up frozen dinners, the brand names jumping under the fluorescence on the bright, stacked up packages. She would have to pilfer her earthquake supplies or stop at Kentucky Fried Chicken and buy little broken legs and breasts. The cat had food; the room would darken around him until it was the same color as his fur.

She sat down on a bench facing the ocean. *Think.* There were certain minutes on earth when nothing was right, as if time were scarred and stuck in its conveyor belt. She took out the malathion flyer. Information could help you out or do you in. She had asked very little about the cellist. It was easier, after all the years of candor melting into silences into lying, simply to leave.

She skimmed:

No warning to pregnant women   bees should be taken away   for seven days   put cars in garage   the bait is not supposed to drip from the trees but   heat inversion twilight   fine chemical mist over the valley   highly toxic when inhaled and sprayed into the air   discovered malathion is the same company developed gas used by the Nazis in the

She looked out at the ocean.

gas chambers

There was an extremist group now that insisted the Holocaust had never happened, the unspeakable attempting to replace the unthinkable, assassins of memory.

uncontrollable coughing   chest pains   extreme fatigue paralysis   conjunctivitis   rare diseases   He told me to go to hell   in heavy amounts   uphill   the wind blowing from that direction   no longer able to do much loss of memory before I was in excellent health

She noticed that she was walking toward the car.

◾

Farther north, every once in a while, there was something, a rape, a murder; the nearer beaches were safer. She had to think of that now that she was alone. If she drove up Route 1 just so far she would be fine. She would do that for herself. That would be something.

The nude beach was the most beautiful, with acres of leafy brussels sprouts spreading right up to the edge of the cliff, but she would avoid it because she might run into a student there. She already had, once. She had been wearing pants and a shirt and had kept her eyes on his face but he had looked down at her body twice as if a second glance might make her clothes disappear. He had been in the humanities class, the author of a paper on Kafka that began *Gregor Samsa awoke one morning to find himself in a no-win situation.* Pascal, with his infinite spaces, had given him trouble too. Incredibly, for a moment, she could remember some of the famous passage, *Man is only a reed . . . a puff of smoke, a drop of water is enough to kill him. . . . All our dignity, then, consists in thought. It is upon this that we must depend, not on space and time, which we would not in any case be able to fill.*

She had forgotten to fill the gas tank. the gauge read close to empty, and she passed up the detour through the stand of eucalyptus she and Nick had always visited on the way to San Francisco. Long strips of pink and gray bark peeled down the trees in narrow maps of damage. The young eucalyptuses were fragile in a storm. The best thing to be in an earthquake was flexible. Had she wanted to be hurt? No, but after years of hurt she had wanted his guilt made evident, justice served. He had grown less and less fair to her.

Yet she knew that in the ruthless order of nature there was no justice. Miles north at Año Nuevo Beach every winter the huge elephant seals coupled in the water and later the leftover males hunkered down on the beaches, slithering up the low, sandy cliffs, heaving their tonnage onto the new pups, raping them and often killing them with their weight, the pups squealing in fear and pain. She and Nick had seen this on a tour, a group of ten people yelling and yelling at the bull seal till he rolled off the shaking pup, taking his time, till they left. But if there were no justice, how had anyone thought of it in the first place?

She turned into a small parking area and got out of the car, breathing in the large pungent smell of the ocean. The waves were letting things go and letting things in as if it were possible to turn your life into something different at any moment. Before last year's 5.2 there had been an arch at this beach. Now there was only a cliff, the surf smashing out a hundred paintings, the colors of cameo, nicotine, mahogany, rich and wet, in the wall of the rock.

Laura saw only two people on the beach at the end of the trail. Two girls, their bodies firm as bombs, spoke in Los Angeles accents. Their vowels seemed to have irrigation ditches inside them. "I feel real gude now," one was saying. "But like I was going out with him for three months, okay? And so I go, basically, I don't think I want to go out with you anymore? I mean, he just said like, 'Really,' in a totally nasty way?"

Laura took off her sandals and scrunched through the cool sand. A woman partly draped in a towel was posing for photographs next to the pampas grass growing out of the cliff, her blondeness matched to the feathery platinum blooms, her skin shockingly smooth against the protruding textures of rock. Somewhere a bird Laura couldn't identify was crying *rigid digit rigid digit*. On this side of the beach the sea sounded tiny, distant, and cozy; back near the path it had been a flat roar. If Nick lied and she didn't remember, could it matter? Was her forgetting a kind of forgiving?

Laura felt a presence on the empty beach. A man sat cross-legged on the sand in a deep niche in the cliff; he was bearded and wore swimming trunks, his eyes closed, his fingers curved in a *mudra*. Often people came to the beach to do yoga, tai chi, meditation; there were organized classes on the beaches closer to town. Willow had told her that if you sit in a cave at the ocean you get an

idea of what to do with your life. The man looked pale and spiritual. He was uttering a low nasal drone — Laura couldn't make
out the words — a mantra, a way of getting sound on your side.

She found herself breathing more deeply as she walked past. A
small waterfall glistened down copper-streaked rock into a shallow pool, a waterfall she had thought was on a different beach
where there were rocks with fossils as extinct as memory. Growing out of the cliffside next to the waterfall were snapdragons
stippled red on their yellow tongues, like dots on the delicate
flesh of a lobster. Laura stared at the waterfall until the rocks next
to it seemed to flow upward. Underneath the hushed cascade of
the waterfall were the reassuring explosions of surf, the waves
breathing into spray. She felt herself loosening as she listened to
the indrawn roaring breath of the ocean, the push of breath out
again. All she needed was to hear the breathing of the ocean and
to see another person occasionally, doing something wholesome
and attentive, and she would be fine.

A man was coming toward her as she approached the end of
the beach that was narrowing with the incoming tide, almost
close enough to step on her shadow. He wore a cracked leather
jacket and blue jeans greenish from dirt and wear. His skin and
his eyes looked as if he had slept facedown in a campsite full of
trash, and he dragged a German shepherd across the sand on a
leash wrapped almost to his fist, the dog skidding on its back
legs. Laura felt her body break up into chunks of fear, disgust,
pity; she was as helpless to rescue the dog as she had been with
the elephant seal. She passed him, poking her elbows out to her
sides to look tough, and then turned to walk yards behind
him; she did not want to be alone at that end of the beach.
He hadn't looked at her, lost in some world of acid or crack or
speed. She thought of the pale man in the shallow cave, his calm.
Those were the extremes of living here — the inoffensive con-
templatives or the men whose dogs slid sideways in the backs

of their pickup trucks as they screeched around hairpin curves.

She walked with small steps and let the man get far ahead of her. The cave might be empty by now, made warm by the contemplative, and she could sit there, safe and breathing. Or she would sneak a look at him as she passed even though you were supposed to look away if someone sat very still, revering the earth and its mysteries.

As she approached she saw that the man's eyes were closed but his position had changed slightly. He had made a zero with his thumb and middle finger. Now he lengthened the zero, made it with a loose fist, his hand a rhythm pumping up and down at the center of his body, his swim trunks gone. She was sick before she realized, then the shock sent the blood rushing to her face. She walked fast, not seeing, a dizzy feeling traveling across her heart. Willow would be with Thor now, melting him away from the doomed woman; Steve was at his cousin's, eating brown rice and dhal, comfortable in a way Laura could barely imagine. The maggoty whiteness of the man's body was like an obscenity on a wall.

She sat down as close as she could to the Los Angeles girls. A Labrador, heavy with health, frisked around them. One of the girls, breezy, chattering, unhitched the top of her bathing suit. "Don't!" Laura said. "There's some guy back there —" A half gesture was enough to make the girl blush — her innocence flushed out of hiding into her face — and refasten the strip of flowered cotton.

"Unreal," the girl said. Then they moved away nervously, clapping for the dog. The other girl tossed a small stick, and the dog ran, skidded, licked it from the air, galloped back to her.

Laura had looked like the girls one hundred years ago. Firm, as if she belonged on *terra firma*. If Nick had been with her he would have looked and looked at the girls, and she would have looked away from his looking. He would have blinked wildly, trying to force some false indifference into his eyes. How could someone be right for you but not good for you? Nothing supported her now except mother earth, and how quickly that was giving way — nitrates, formaldehyde, malathion, DBCB, EDB, DDT, PCBs, CFCs. The earth was still the place where you buried your dead but now it was also one of the dying.

Were the choppers overhead at this very minute, stuttering a hundred feet above her garden, spraying poison, the garden withering backward to a time before Eden? Eve's first disobedience and the fruit, you don't make a mistake like that twice. Willow would tell her to find her sacred task, her place in the universe among exploding stars, a dying sun, debris and rubble in the earth's penumbra. Should she call the police? How far was the nearest phone?

The wind came up suddenly, scattering birds as if they were leaves. The northern beaches grew cold in the late afternoons. Laura's blouse flapped and sand stung her face. She had read somewhere that air anywhere could be from over 200 miles away. It gave her a feeling of strangers.

Her legs were shaky on the uphill path. Twice she looked over her shoulder. When she slammed herself shut in the car, panting hard, the silence seemed unnatural after the roar of the ocean and wind. She smoothed her hair, and in the rearview mirror saw, on a station wagon across the lot, a license plate that said, TOUCH ME. *Unreal.* A woman was in the station wagon, adjusting a baby seat; then she went around to the driver's side.

The wind stopped for a moment; the trees outside were still. Now she could hear it. The dream last night had been about a wind that didn't belong to her. She saw her antique dresser with the lace runner on top, and on the lace runner were a small turquoise bear, a rock with a fossil snail iced into it, and pink pebbles from a distant ocean. Nick was there, looming over the dresser, and with enormous force he blew all the objects onto the floor, the lace crumpled and blown off too. The top of her dresser was blank and bare and she could feel the powerful wind of his breath as bitter and frightened sounds came from her throat, separate from any voice she knew in herself.

"What am I doing?" he said to her, his voice huge in the dream, and she replied timidly — she could hear the words muffle and blow as if she were in a big wind — "You're blowing on me," the flat taste of her obedience in her mouth. Her hand shook on the ignition key. To re-member is to put back together, then you fall apart, amnesia's Valium gone.

She stared straight ahead and saw the Los Angeles girls, who had reached the crest of the path from the beach. At a party years ago, not her kind of party, she had glimpsed Nick in strobe light on a sofa between two girls in shiny dresses, hems high on the thigh that year. Her memory clicked shut like a camera finished with a picture, but she forced it open and found the cellist embedded in a transparency over the girls. Hindsight gave the clarity of second sight. There was only one thing worse than the end and that was the beginning of the end.

And yet he had loved her many days of her life after that, as if they existed in a strobe effect of separate gestures, no continuity, no consequence. The last good day together had been only two years ago. They had gone to visit the house in New Hampshire. The few houses that had once been there, wooden houses, had melted into the trees, pine against pine in the midst of the light and shade and stone walls. Now the house was no longer there and the road wound through tract houses set into the landscape like potted plants. They drove ten miles to their old swimming pond, where insects played a game of jacks on the water and trees tossed their reflections onto the surface like flowers. She held his hand and let the sun shine on her face, her loose blouse lifted by the wind. She wore nothing underneath and the sun was warm on her breasts. He kissed her neck and lifted her blouse, their minds clear and peaceful together; he spread a blanket on the ground.

She released the hand brake, pulled out of her space, and saw, guiltily, the yellow wheelchair painted on the asphalt; had she imagined, unconsciously, that she was entitled to it? TOUCH ME was in front of her as she turned out of the lot. She wanted to put her head on the woman's shoulder and go to sleep. You could pretend that here and there people were caring for you, blessed seconds of comfort, because where was the softness of mother earth? She and Nick had made love quietly for hours in a grove of birches next to the pond, needly pines exhaling into their skin and hair, the soft water of sunlight on their skin, a scattering of tiny bluets under them, a blessing from the sky as it rushed through green leaves. Better not to remember the Chinese boxes of greater and greater happiness. TOUCH ME pulled out and passed the car in front of it; Laura, for a split second, felt abandoned.

She drove slowly, watching out of the corner of her eye how the wind dragged the dark water into wavelets and cut it up into small pieces of white. She had to get home. She didn't want to see the changeable desires of sunset, pinks and mauves straining for climax until moonlight shattered like glass on the breakers. She felt a long shiver when she thought of the man in the cave, the image of him like larvae in the seams of her clothes.

She glanced down at the pretty yellow cotton dress she had worn for Steve. When would Nick call about the piano? Her dashboard clock would tell her nothing; it gave the same time always. Her gas tank read empty; she knew that with her car that was also a lie, but she didn't know where the truth began.

A helicopter smacked its *whop whop* into the air over the beach, but the ocean was calmer now. The evenness of the waves slipping slowly into the night reminded her of Willow's voice. You can live a new way if you sing a new song, Willow had told her as she hummed at the spa, upside down on one of the machines, the humming blowing her blonde hair forward. Nick couldn't stand to hear anyone hum. Laura began to hum a small tune, her breathing deepening. Singing near water increased your second sight.

Laura drove past the stand of eucalyptuses. The small ones were fragile but the big ones, once they were well established, were strong enough to withstand the wind. The good was as true as the bad, if you waited. A turn of the light, a temperature change, hope comes out of nowhere, where was the justice in that? Willow's voice wandered into her mind again. *The best thing to do, if you have amnesia, is to become clairvoyant.* She laughed, her laughter sounding unfamiliar to her. She imagined the phone ringing, Steve calling, concerned, to check on how she was, her shaky voice telling him about the man on the beach, her voice getting stronger, telling him everything that was on her mind.

She turned on her lights, twin beams pulling the darkening road toward her. She saw, distinctly — the image as sharp as what Willow must have seen of Yosemite — a day in autumn, season of acceptable little deaths, the leaves red on the maple and liquidambar, a day when there would finally be a change, everything in balance inside her. She would be in the living room, the piano gone, listening to the Saturday opera live from the Met, the music that was passé for Nick now, music he had tossed away like Kleenex. The members of the audience would be roaring for curtain calls as if they were in pain. Singers in elaborate costumes she couldn't see would come out and take bow after bow until the diva was left alone in applauded solitude under the lights, the tears streaming down her cheeks and flowers filling her flawless arms. Laura would be petting the cat. And amnesia would be part of it: She could see that one Saturday in October, her body filled with music, her eyes clear, she would not remember that, right now, at the edge of her mind and exhausted, she was sure she was driving into the empty summer nights of the rest of her life.

Under Malathion

WAKE UP in the July heat and turn on the radio, the warblers already going outside. KFAT announces that it's Linda Ronstadt's birthday, plays a few. Linda's thirty-five today, a face like a baby's ass, a great voice. Then the news comes on, there's an assonant rhythm in the rich voice of the commentator this morning Alameda, malathion, Santa Clara, malathion, malathion. Areas 1 to 4, just over the low mountains from here, receiving spraying on Wednesday, Tuesday, Friday, and Thursday. And then there are call-ins: "Are you saying malathion has something to do with *nerve* gas?"

I turn off KFAT and try to think about my last vacation, Zion National Park, trees the color of watercress and rugged cliffs ruddy as roast beef. And Bryce Canyon, Fanny Brice Canyon, one of many national parks named after great comedians. A couple of weeks ago I drove up the coast to take a walk on Jack Benny Beach but there was no one there except a tall man who was sweeping the sand with a broom, not wearing a uniform. A jogger's body had been discovered on the next beach, a woman naturally, a month earlier. From the overlook at Eddie Cantor Chasm I saw him, a thin figure bent like a wizard over a caldron, sweeping. The wind was hard, riding in like a chopper, a Harley-

Davidson wind, over the waves. The eucalyptus slowed their round young blue-dusted leaves.

I've spent the last six days with women teaching at a writing conference for women. Men began to look strange to me, welcome but strange. I thought of Bambi's mother raising her delicate sniffer in alarm and crying "Man!" into the dappled light and shade of the Disney forest. "Man!" and they all run.

Benita, the other teacher, and I took an hour out to have dinner at a local restaurant instead of at the cafeteria. We sipped our mint tea. She said, "I heard a rumor that Celestial Seasonings has been bought by Nestlé's."

"I hate rumors," I said, and then on second thought, "Maybe we should send the tea back, talk to them about thousands of babies dead of powdered formula, mothers told their own milk isn't good enough."

"We can write letters," she said, as the waiter arrived. I look with wonder at his beautiful red beard, how it springs, just like that, out of his handsome cheeks and chin.

We talk about men; it's as if we're talking about strains of flu, how to take care of ourselves and so on. Benita declares that the food we eat is made up of things that are killing us. "There are sixty dangerous pesticides," she says, "legally allowed in the food we put in our mouths." Like royalty it seems we are being poisoned slowly. Anorexia nervosa isn't a psychosis, it's a political disease.

Benita and I eat our vegetarian entrées and get sentimental about living animals. We agree that creatures really do it for us, that seeing a covey of quail crossing the road, a mother quail and eleven babies, a pale, pebbled moon up in the early morning sky, can make our day. Benita tells me how she was sitting in her living room one day when a stag stepped up onto the deck and then slowly walked into the house and lay down, looking as if he had plucked his antlers from a knotty pine wall above a fireplace.

They just sat together for a while, the two of them, she being really quiet so he wouldn't feel threatened, and then the doorbell startled him and he sprang up and clattered off the deck.

"How marvelous," I say. "But also, I'd be nervous. Now a doe might be different —"

"It's because of the women's conference," she says. "The antlers scare you."

I make a point of thinking how lovely it would be, all the way home — the antlers like a philodendron, sculpting space in the living room, the quietness of that privileged moment. Then I feel something touching the back of my neck, some consciousness, and I notice I'm being tailed by two guys in a green pickup. I pull over into a well-lit driveway where two people are kissing good night in a car with the motor running, and watch the pickup pass slowly, then rev up with a nasty roar, no longer stalking prey. The woman gets out of the car and glares at me.

On my last day at the women's conference a student presents a piece she has written about images in the media. She talks about a book she read that shows how admen fill photographs with ghost images — subliminal skulls and bones in ice cubes in liquor glasses (because heavy drinkers want to die), and obscenities, faint and barely discernible to the conscious eye, on the faces and bodies of alluring women. She was one of them, she says, in the long modeling career she has since abandoned. She goes on to show us more images from the media, Xeroxes of photos from *Hustler* magazine, a woman with her head held over a toilet bowl, her hair snarled back painfully in a man's hand, her face in a smile. Many of the students look sick, and stunned, and frightened. They also, kindly, worry about the slenderness of the woman writing these pieces, and hope that she has the stamina for her enterprise.

That same afternoon I find in my mailbox an article written by a man I have recently met, about the destruction of obscene photographs in the university library by a local feminist. He differs with her act of civil disobedience and says, besides, he found the photos of a voluptuous nude lying in a puddle of blood exciting. He says that when he discovered that the puddle of blood was actually maple syrup he found it amusing. I remember the model that morning reading aloud to us about the moment she had perceived the subliminal writing, an unmistakable obscenity written on her own open American face. I cancel my plans to see the man later in the week because he confuses sex and death — reason enough.

When the women's conference is over I sleep all day and get up to prepare a tranquil dinner. I decide to read *Madame B. Ovary* again while I wait for the rice to cook, to see what Flaubert is up to. I need the balance of those sentences to keep me from thinking too much about the article the man sent me until I can think more clearly. Then from the living room I hear noises in the kitchen and realize the mice are back. I hate mice, they make me shriek and they don't belong anywhere; they were put on this earth as moving food, fast food for hawks and owls. I scoop up my lazy cat and go into the kitchen where I learn the meaning of the noise and of the noun *stranger:* a snake is slithering down from under the door of the cabinet below the sink — phallic revenge for a week among women. I race forward instinctively, though frightened, hoping to behead him with the door.

I press my knee against the door after I've slammed it, tremble there for several minutes, and then fetch the enormous one-volume *Oxford English Dictionary* to lean against it. I used to look up tiny Emily Dickinson words in that hugeness. I remember her snake poem, the one that ends "and zero at the bone." I look down and see that he has withdrawn, and I dial my nearest neighbor, my hand trembling as he listens carefully and then says brightly, "Kundalini! Wow!" He puts his girlfriend on, she was raised in the desert, and she says, "If it comes back and it's a rattler, don't move and it won't hurt you." Advice to Victorian wives.

The next day I call the animal rescue service. The snake could have been a rattler; I've seen them outside here. Although gopher snakes do puff out their faces to look triangular, in imitation. But was it triangular? I can't remember, and didn't see enough of its body to check for diamonds. I know snakes have skin like rose petals, very dry and delicate, and rid us of mice, but I was once in a snake house on feeding day, and still remember the squeals of the Easter chicks ready in pans of twenty-four waiting for their transformation from their own lives into someone else's food. The way a woman plus maple syrup becomes a pancake.

The woman at the rescue service finally picks up the phone. "We rescue animals, not people from animals," she says. "Why don't you just call a neighbor?"

"Why don't I just feed it candy till its fangs fall out," I say, and hang up.

KFAT says, "It is not necessary to evacuate the area. Pregnant women should stay indoors during aerial spraying." Helicopters tracking prey. "Take special precaution and wash children, keep toys inside." Keep pets inside. The malathion will come from above, like Skylab, like Chicken-Licken. The sky is falling, don't lick anyone who's been outside. A rattler's venom digests its prey. I remember they mate by lying prone for hours, the male inserting his hemipenes.

Benita calls, she's in spray area four. "I think I'll give up jogging. I don't want to run around in that stuff. Anyway, jogging's not fun anymore, it's all too ideological." She advises me to think of the snake as a sacred instructor, "teach and be taught," to remember those *zaftig* Cretan goddesses who wear snakes around their necks the way women used to wear ermine, or feather boas. We talk about our grandmothers, fur coats, our mothers, dresses, the way we were raised as women. "You know," she says, "I was brought up to be polite. I never imagined I'd have to think about the death of the planet."

I decide to put Brillo in the mouse holes and to forget about the snake, to leave it to the reptile brain coiled at the top of my spine, to keep my mammal brain clear of concern. I remember to turn a page on the elegant Japanese calendar given to me by one of the students. It seems to be a new week. Under the waxing moon I dream about an owl, and it's an owl that wakes me, for a minute, at three a.m. His feathery *hou hou*s quiver in the tree outside the window. I jot something down in the dark on the pad I keep next to my bed, and in the morning, when I wake up, as relaxed as if I'd shaken out all my feathers too, I find it there. "It is heaven and earth to be a lower animal," I read. So I open the sliding door to let in the morning air. Area four is over the mountains but right here it looks very clear.

The Man with the Blues Guitar:
A Progression on Poetry and Music

I T'S APRIL IN SANTA CRUZ, the tail end of the Northern
California rainy season, and a composer she knows wants her
to come north to San Francisco to be part of a panel discus-
sion on poetry and music in a pleasant performance space in
the heart of the city. She decides to take part, and to make her
contribution in the form of a poem, a poem that will have chords
in it, a poem that will conceal the fact that it's a poem. But her
concentration keeps dissolving in the gloomy inundations of a
week of rain, a week preceded by the inundations of a month
of rain, and in the trouble a man in her life is giving her, or as
John Cage says, "The more you're with musicians, the crazier
you get."

Day after day she goes into her study, trying to find the poem,
but nothing comes. Then finally one afternoon the sun appears,
holds on, a first line comes to her, another comes, then another
line, then the *thud thud* of a bass guitar, the neighbor's stereo,
finds her, someone else's blood thumping in her veins, trespass
so complete there is no place to hide. She wants to write a poem
that will pull the inaudible out of the audible, a poem that

will bring her audience peace, but it isn't quite enough for her to do it.

She turns to her record collection and puts on a record at random, in self-defense and as an omen, the way she would cut the Tarot or consult the I Ching. She hears the anorexic minutiae of disco, feels it tighten her pulses, and she dances for several minutes. Then she sits in front of the stereo and puts on one record after another, drowning out the neighbor's sound, waiting for a sign. She listens to the predictable unnerving undertow of reggae, the philosulfuric Rolling Stones, piano rills drowning in a golden lake of trombones, a jug band whose lead singer sounds as if he's swallowing his tongue, Keith Jarrett's arpeggios like runny egg white, Marianne Faithfull's broken-dolly voice, the Bleach Boys, a saxophone that slides its hand over the world with obsessional devotion, giving way to the copacetic hiccup of a more avant-garde saxophone and its muffled, huffing bleat, then sixteen conga drummers, all Moslems so it sounds like a single drum. She stumbles on the hits of the fifties, a generation of music that milked every platitude of high-school heartache — no poetry, only music, then . . . Who was that singing? The Pomades? The Questionnaires?

It begins to rain again, she puts on a series of rainy-day-ain't-got-no-lovin' blues, only half-listening, trying to find the poem — is it Fiddlin' Blind Lightnin' Junior Sonny Boy Smith, or what, singing, *She asked for water, he gave her gasoline?* Is it Big Sister Little Mama Johnson doing that shouting, or is it the falsetto of Little Walter Walker? *Blues is truth,* said Brownie McGhee, *blues is not a dream. If you've got no love to give, don't give it to me,* says a good woman singer. She likes to listen to women singers, so she gives in, chooses Billie Holiday as she always does, sure that long ago, in her crib, she heard that drug-roughened voice, over the radio no face or cocaine-white gardenia visible, a snowdrift outside the window, her young mother washing the dishes in snowy suds. The caressive voice had sealed her in then, had made her safe: she had no idea the voice was singing about suffering.

And she herself sang, very early, she remembers, sang and sang after an appendectomy, wouldn't stop singing until they gave her piano lessons at the age of seven, a long career in music abbreviated however because Mr. Bissell crept his hand under her blouse, working his way in through the sleeve as she practiced a simple rondo in the red-covered book, until finally she stopped, pleading boredom to her blissfully ignorant mother, starting piano lessons again later with Mrs. Hallowell, eighty years old, who fell asleep before the scales were finished and whose elderly vagueness was echoed in her love for the pedal from which her foot never rose, *homp homp,* be it ever so humble there's no place like *homp homp,* Mrs. Hallowell leaving her earthly home forever one day while instructing another student, end of music until at fifteen she put a tenor sax in her mouth for the first time in the class that was open to everyone, the teacher telling a latecomer, "Here's how you try out for the class. I'll play two notes and you tell me which is higher," and the teacher banged out a C and the kid said, "That's higher," and the teacher said, "You're in, kid." Which reminded her of John Cage's anecdote about playing the Buddhist mass for a class at the New School one note over and over for fifteen minutes until one of the students rose, screaming, "I can't stand another minute of it," and Cage mercifully leaned over to take the needle from the record and another student called out, "I was just getting used to it." Which reminded her of her favorite joke in which there are three hermits sitting in a cave and one day a horse gallops past the mouth of the cave and a month later one of the hermits says, "Hey that was a beautiful brown horse that ran past the mouth of the cave," and a couple of months later the second hermit says, "That was no brown horse, that was a white one," and a year later the third hermit says, "If you don't stop this bickering, I'm leaving." When she told the new man in her life the joke he told her with a serious face he'd have to think about it.

She turned off the stereo. The rain sounded like handfuls of seeds angrily hurled onto the roof. From the neighbor's house there was silence. She was interested in qualities of silence, silence like a series of hyphens, silence like the weeping of creatures without eyes, mammal silence, the silence of fish, and the silence of humans, which depended on how they were breathing. There wasn't any such thing as silence of course, if you understood that there wasn't only the sound a thing or being makes but the sound a thing or being *is,* its dimensions and vibrations in the space around it. This intrinsic sound was different from adhesive or illustrative sound, that is, the sound a being uses to get our attention, to perpetuate itself, to draw itself into the future.

They were agreed, he and she, that they didn't have a future. They were not in love; love is when you automatically correct the inexact intervals before you actually hear them. Still, when she tried to concentrate on poetry and music, on avoiding the melody hopefully, he was the bass line that interfered. It was only a few months ago that she had sat on his low sofa and looked at him as he stood above her, slightly swaybacked compared to the acoustic hunch of a folksinger, the bass guitar held across his pelvis and aimed to one side like a gun, an intravenous cord trailing from it and ending in a plug on the wall. He told her she was the first to hear the riffs and phrases he'd invented that afternoon for his "Flying to New York Change at Chicago Blues," and she told him she had never been so close to a bass before, it was like being close to an elephant, the bigness booming through her. Because he was so attractive she submitted to the loudness of the seduction, wondering if the price of this connection would be mutation: She did not believe that anything so loud and deep could leave her unchanged. She moved to a different place on the sofa, onto some bulging springs: Probably there was only one spot that was fatal. Somewhere she had read that the right music could freeze water, or kill a man.

They talked and talked. He told her that when he heard a tune he heard the harmony line just as strongly, and she understood that, whether he knew it or not, he was telling her about the other women in his life. He told her that sound as it exists in time is rhythm, and rhythm is the mood of time. For repetition you had to have conviction, and all keepers of the rhythm, bass or drum, were keepers of the flame. Sometimes she asked him avid questions but lost the answers while looking at his good-looking face. Leo de Fender, she seemed to remember, invented the bass guitar in the early fifties as a weapon. De Fender was the first to understand the relationship between rhythm and aggression. Because of its shotgun-length neck and its role in causing deafness, the bass inspired a series of local guitar-control laws, phased out in the seventies. She wondered whatever happened to the big double bass they hugged from behind, humble and barely audible. "They put it on its side," he said, "tensed it till it got electric." No longer encircled like a woman, now it was held far away from the heart, taking the old chords with it but propelling them so far it could drive you crazy. She thought of the several neighbors she'd moved away from because of those chords.

She tried to convince him of the balancing value of quietness. "Jimi Hendrix was the first to play loud, right?" she asked him, "and he died, right?" She talked up a sense of acoustic proportion, the logic of electric companies charging customers according to the volume: The louder the stereo the higher the bill. She lectured him about music in the space heater age: "We could dance all winter to keep warm," she said, "the way bees do. Rilke said poets are bees of the invisible. We could dance to keep the invisible warm." She spoke to him of the greatness of poetry, showed him Wallace Stevens's "Man with the Blues

Guitar," *sic,* and he propped up her thoughts on music and poetry by taking her dancing at most of the venues in town. They went to hear The Clap, a New Wave group, at the Civic, and she looked at the amps and thought, yes, we are dancing with *machines.*

They went to Sam's in San Jose, a vast cowboy redneck heaven with hurricane lamps and wagon wheel chandeliers, listened to Prince Ida with a metal washboard hung like a bib around his neck, Zydeco's son running two spoons up and down the ridges in zigzag rhythms as if he were stroking himself, gleeful as a baby. There was no doubt about it — music was better physical exercise than poetry.

The bass guitarist hadn't yet begun the push-pulling of her then, push-pull like a diatonic accordion, unnerving her through the unpredictable slowing and speeding up of his attention. They made love to the Who, to Taj Mahal, to seven rounds of Dylan singing "Tangled Up in Blue," heating his underheated room with their bodies for most of the rainy winter. *You really turn me on,* he told her, is not an acoustic expression. He trusted her enough to confide that he once thought the Beatles were brothers, but no further. She could hear him thinking, Now what do I do? She assured him that it isn't where it's going, it's where it's coming from. Once you admit there's no particular ending, everything changes. "No music ever ends," said Duke Ellington. "Everything I care for happens all the time," said a poet she likes to read. "I was just getting used to it," said the student about the Buddhist mass. Although one did have to distinguish: Marcel Duchamp's phrase *finally unfinished* was not the same as *eternally undone.*

She left her house, stopped at the Hotel St. Joze for a cappuccino, and headed for the pier. A bumper sticker on the car ahead of her said, IF IT'S TOO LOUD, YOU'RE TOO OLD. It was raining lightly. She looked for seals in the dark choppy waters around the pilings. She thought she heard a foghorn, single ghostnote of a bass guitar, the underbelly of things. The gray whales were out there somewhere, dreaming in bulk, forty or fifty dreams between soundings, singing their songs in sleep and waking. There was one kind of whale that had a nine-movement song, and over time the song gradually altered until after ten years of yawing from a given tune nothing was the same as in the original, with whales of this kind all over the world amending their songs simultaneously. Telepathy, she thought, arises as a means of preserving culture in conditions of diaspora. Computers were corporate simulations of telepathy, but for whales the telepathic songs were a form of prayer, each note an invocation to a diety they could understand.

She did believe that poetry and music were twins in prayer in the beginning, devotions driving the gods down into the heart, spinning them into our cells. Music wasn't difficult to learn then, with harps from the bones and hair of mastodons, tempi based on the rhythm of running hooves, and chants, to deepen the breathing, bring oxygen to the blood, song giving the fire for labor, or becoming an incantation that taunted the tribal dark. Gulls swooped and yawped and her mind began to clear as the rain thinned out to a drizzle. She imagined her body as fields of sound in order to see how she felt in every part of herself, to find where the static was, the secret thresholds and securest places. She asked herself avid questions. What notes have you heard today? For as the wise composer Azebub Sobelow said, "The shape of your mind is the shape of your daily music." She asked herself, in a Fascist state, which is more dangerous, poetry or music? She wondered, what singer had said, give me a peach or a pear 'cuz you know it's been cold? She wondered, which is more efficient in postponing death, music or poetry? Sex was a deep postponer of death, and she thought of the sounds of courtship, ranging from the sweetest of human murmurs to the yelping of hyenas, mating only every couple of years with acrimonious brevity. She wondered, if the spiral was the essential pattern in nature, what was the essential sound? She wondered, would she ever be able to write a poem that wasn't a poem, a mating of the inaudible and the audible that came across as a chord? The sky cleared for a minute. She heard no bass line; nowhere was there the unpredictable undertow of his guitar. Everything she cared for happened all the time, but what if she stopped caring, even though she was just getting used to it? As the clouds began to shred away she remembered that for the last several nights she had been dreaming about music. She unearthed the dreams easily as the sky brightened the silence around her — a dream of Easter music rising like bread as the choir sang, another of the silvery unplaceable song of a two-year-old, another a nightmare stuffed with the sounds made by swans and giraffes with broken necks, sounds full of anger at the bass guitarist, another where she sat dropping a wad of paper on a bongo drum from a distance of three feet, the weak feeling of waiting for him to call, but the best one and the longest was a dream where *ah dah dah* was hummed again and again, giving a breathy background to a pure melodious lead, guiding her to a place where a crowd of people cried, "Where are the saxophones? Where are the saxophones?" and a singer came up to her singing, "No matter what, it ain't gonna look nothin' but like a poem," and she nodded in the dream, and agreed with him.

What Is Lost, What Is Missing, What Is Gone:
Scenes After the Earthquake

THE FIRST TIME I was hit by lightning, brilliant flash, deafening crack and boom, I split like a tree, and all the voices inside me, fragments of the true story of the nervous system, became audible, pleasant company at times, but sometimes so distracting I can't remember what I mean to say.

I brought the voices with me when I left the forests of Santa Cruz for the built-over desert of San Diego to teach at a campus of pink windowless cubes and hula palms with their skirts of shade.

They say it's the unsettled ones, the wanderers, who are able to ascend to the highest rung of the soul's ladder, but leaving Santa Cruz was the deepest sacrifice, a kind of death. The town isn't small, yet somehow you can hold all of it in your mind at once, and it was always flowing inside me, sloping toward the sea, bends in the road rounded by a sequence of acacia trees, the paler and paler walls of evergreen in the mountain valley I lived in — the landscape laying down its subtle patterns and circulation in my body, smoothing its green hills and deep slopes into me even as I slept.

Trees that have already been shattered attract lightning. In the forest near my house in Santa Cruz, a house that is still mine, the redwoods are furrowed and blackened from a century of electrical storms. Higher, far away, the bristlecone pines — the most ancient trees on earth, where Michael and I ended our marriage — are sculpted by lightning's fire into the burnt sienna and ivory elegies of trees stripped bare.

The word that comes to mind is *loss*.

■

"Inhale along with me," I tell the roomful of writing students, leading them in breathing exercises it's better to do when the air isn't brown. Beyond the pink buildings is a heavy curtain of smog, the four-letter word no one will use.

"People stop feeling real when they can't breathe," I explain. I think about Santa Cruz, the air so clear there. "Write about loss," I say. "A person or place. Something lost, missing, gone." It's 5:04: The dark leaves of the clock's hands reach for the right side of its face. The second hand, like a sewing machine stitching a circle, goes *tszk, tszk.*

I've been hit twice, disproving the adage. Once in a summer cottage when we were splitting up I closed the window to keep out the rain, and lightning — spectacular, speechless — shocked me from the tips of my hair to the soles of my feet. The second time was in Yosemite, when we tried again. Zigzagging along the John Muir river trail under the thunderheads, I was drunk with fear till I got to the car, and seconds after I'd leapt inside a bolt hit my door in a burst of light. *Be here now,* the voices said.

1

After class I drive home into the sunset's blitz of magentas, the hot Santa Ana winds crawling along my nerves. Blank-faced condos bite into the hillsides, zones of defeat that shut down the heart. If I were in Santa Cruz I'd be meeting Shep and Molly for our Tuesday movie. I'd stop at the Coffee Roasting Company, browse in Bookshop Santa Cruz, use the old-fashioned bathroom on the second floor of Ford's, and meet them for dinner at India Joze before we went on to the Nickelodeon to see a foreign film we'd argue about later over ice cream. Now they are renting my small house in the mountains, taking care of my things. I'm a spider who has dropped down on her filament and can't get back to her web.

Can't get back to her wet, one of the voices says.

The rains begin right around now in Santa Cruz, ushering in the humanizing gravities of autumn. But here, at 70 degrees, it's dry, noncommittal. I switch on the radio, longing for more than the local, just as the Jaguar in front of me, GRT LIF, swerves two lanes over without signaling. It has not been a GRT LIF for a long time now, marriage gone, jobs hard to come by, bad luck, Santa Cruz the only consolation. Someone on NPR is saying that East Germany has kicked out Honecker after eighteen years. The cheezy billboards and jerry-built stucco houses whiz by. MES-DUP, JOKAH, and CANDO all pass me in the middle lane. License plots, koans of the road. Then the radio drifts to an adjacent station and the voice sounds too excited to be official:

"It's a big one. The World Series. It's a seven point one."

I begin to shiver, though the inside of the car is baking hot.

"In San Francisco."

Ice cubes avalanche down my back.

"The epicenter's ten miles north of Santa Cruz. It was rush hour," the excited voice says.

I race to get home, racing to keep up with the eight-lane stream of traffic roaring around me. Blind to the road I see my house in its peaceful nest of live oak and madrone, ten miles north of Santa Cruz. My heart is pounding. Who's alive and who's in a pile of rubble? GRT LIF cuts back in front of me. I can't breathe. In the hot winds, the hot car, I'm like ice.

2

Due to the earthquake in the area you are dialing, your call cannot be completed. Molly, Shep, Dove, Bobby, Grace: Who is alive, hurt, dead? The house could be a shattered heap of lumber, everyone there killed by flying bricks from the old chimney. In August, just before I left, we'd had a 5.2 at one a.m. that sounded like a thousand teeth being pulled out of the earth's mouth as I stumbled toward the doorway in the dark. I'll never get used to the sound of California breaking. The wooden house was flexible as it slid back and forth, back and forth, while I held on to the doorframe. If you live in a stone house, secure and firm, it collapses around you, but wood is good.

Would you could, says some part of my tree.

■

CNN yammers on, loud and rapid, about the World Series and San Francisco. Channel 39 has new information and reverts to a *Jeopardy!* rerun where contestants are frozen in terror. Then the first Santa Cruz pictures appear. They're of Shockley's, with its soft carpets and courtesy, its cases of gold and silver and precious stones, the roof bashed in, beams dangling like broken arms. The place where Michael and I bought our wedding rings.

The quake has destroyed almost all of the downtown gardened promenade, its turn-of-the-century brick and Spanish stucco buildings, its thick fringe of bushes and trees. The promenade was a psychic net where you met friends by chance in the afternoon light that rolled everything in gold batter. It was a focus for the imagination, the closest you could come to sacred ground.

Santa Cruz doesn't know what's happening to them, CNN

says: They're cut off from all communications. Dan Rather, ten channels over, insists in his hollow voice that the Santa Cruz Mountains are uninhabited. I'm mesmerized by the shattered Shockley's, until the pictures from Oakland, seventy miles north, begin to appear. The footage can't stop repeating itself: eighteen blocks of tiered freeway, falling in slow motion, again and again, a dozen times, in the bedroom, killing dozens of people, one by one.

3

The next morning Bobby, old friend of ours, gets through. I've had one hour of sleep, my mind roiling.

His voice trembles on the edge of hysteria. "There've been four hundred aftershocks."

"How far apart are they?"

"Every fifteen minutes: You can feel when they're coming. It's like timing birth pangs. Two of my Queer Nation friends were down from San Francisco. Everyone's sleeping outside." He sounds completely exhausted.

"It's crazy to be outside," I say, "with all the trees."

"No, hon, it's safer. Earthquake instructions are like natural childbirth instructions: When the time comes you do something else. People are afraid to go back into their houses.

"It was like a train coming. First there was rumbling. Then it got louder and stronger and the wall was shot through with cracks. Then Dreamie jumped out the window like a cat from the comics, and I jumped out after her. I could hear the sound of crashing and yelling everywhere. Oh God, here it comes again —"

"Do you want me to try to call later?"

"No, no, keep talking. I'm under a doorway. Your house? I could drive up there, darling, although I don't know." I picture him running his hands through the long silken hair he used to great effect when he was Carmen Monoxide, the bass player in Shep's band. "I don't know. All the way up into the mountains. The roads are like broken zippers. Landslides. I've got to go. They're freaking out in the other doorway. It was my birthday. God, I've known you for ten *years*. I'll try to get hold of Shep. You have to realize, sweetheart, that at five-oh-five the downtown ceased to exist."

4

I spend the next day curled up on the sofa in a nightgown bought on the first floor of Ford's, a nightgown patterned with blue teardrop shapes that look as if they had been wept into the fabric. In front of my San Diego cottage a date palm, paradigm of leisure and paradise, fans itself in the breeze. I've been away from the shady maples of downtown Santa Cruz and the redwoods and pines of the mountains for two months. Every twenty minutes I dial Molly and Shep: There's no recording now, only a silence that sounds as if it had been left out of life itself, a silence that goes on all day and continues into the evening.

Last year, after Molly and I had a tashlich ceremony at Rosh Hashanah, casting our sins in the form of bread into the waves and renewing our Jewishness, we ate apples and honey at my house and coincidentally gave each other Old Testaments, identical volumes of black leather imprinted with gold. I open mine now to the Psalms, and let my prayers waft up to Jehovah, God of my childhood, dispenser of the nectar of justice. To be judged is comforting; you are seen for exactly who you are. In Hebrew, one word, the one root, flowers into *judgment* and *prayer*.

Let my prayer rise before You as the incense, I whisper aloud, my voice made small by so many hours of fear, and as the perfume of my devotions rises in the room, I hear a corresponding whisper like the crackle of parchment, as if an ancient volume were being opened. Then my grandmother, gentle Esther, steps from its pages. The air has her shape, her smell of rose soap, her low voice.

Still with your nose in a book? she says. I laugh, terrified, almost whimpering, as I would if a small wild animal had gotten into the house.

After a disaster you look for mishpocheh, she explains kindly. I can almost see her smooth skin, white petals tinted with rose, her gray eyes more beautiful than any color. She died right after the war. Impossible for her to bear: the piles of skeletons — cousins. The earth outside of Vilna dense with the minerals of kin. Grandma died: It was her quiet way of flinging herself into the pit.

The Inquisition, the Holocaust, those were catastrophes, the Crusades, when they went looking for the Golden Calf, I mean the Holy Grail, running their swords through all the Jews they saw, that was a catastrophe. God willing, no one was killed here, knock wood, a few stores. This is nothing! A downtown! I've seen pictures of Vilna before the war, dark two-story buildings, cobbled streets, stone arches, an urchin, a fruit cart, dozens of synagogues. The Jerusalem of Lithuania when it wasn't the Jerusalem of Poland or Russia.

In Russia we also had earthquakes. We called them pogroms. We would hide in the basement, afraid to breathe. She strokes my hair. For a moment she's a palpable presence, then she recedes to a subliminal hum. In her old age she looked like Madame Curie, the real one, not the movie. She sewed me a lilac taffeta dress when I was seven, slithered it over my lifted arms, the hem-stitches like the footprints of tiny shorebirds. She began to teach me Yiddish, the grandmother tongue: *hershl,* deer; *herzl,* little heart. Patty-cake all fall down on her flowered rug. Fordham Road in the Bronx. The smell of pot roast and mothballs in their small apartment. She gave me an Old Testament Classic Comics, full of colors — Delilah's cheeks, Joseph's coat of ribbony reds and pinks. The sky was Jewish. God, His words in shivery letters, was a genius.

She cradles my face in her hands and draws her other hand gently down my back. *The spine is the palm branch and the heart is the fragrant citron,* she instructs. *Happy Sukkoth.* She looks out the window at the palm tree whose fronds go anywhere in a storm. *You're in a dream! Heat! Hot water! No ax aimed at your head! You don't go to bed at night weeping, terrified. Wake up to this beautiful dream you're in! In the New World we looked for light. Who can blame us, after we were expelled from Spain, the hills of Granada so beautiful with flowering almond trees. The Baltic so cold and overcast: five hundred years of overcoats. The czar saved your life. He hated the Jews: It was because of him and the Cossacks that we left. If we hadn't left because of the pogroms we would have been killed by the Nazis. I can't explain the pines to you, in the woods outside Vilna. We tore up our roots. I was a seamstress in Berlin on my way to marry your grandfather in America. All you need is a needle and thread, you can go anywhere.*

After Esther's death, Grandpa sat in a deep armchair in our living room every Sunday from early afternoon until dinner. He mourned her and everyone lost during the war, his sighs blossoming and expiring through the winter afternoon. It was over now, he knew, as darkness gathered outside the window, but Germany was Gehenna and a Gehenna there would always be.

Go, try them now, Esther says. *Shepherd and Molly and little Dove.* She threads her fingers through my hair. *Still the same curls,* she says.

5

I'm glad it's Shep and Molly who are in my house. Although it takes a surprisingly long time to make a friend in Santa Cruz —

unsettled ground makes for evanescent identities and ephemeral connections — Shep and Molly and I liked each other right away. It's been ten years since I wrote songs for their New Wave group, Missing Children, to prove to myself I wasn't just a part-time academic, a teacher. I wrote the words for their only hit, "What Is Lost, What Is Missing, What Is Gone," and Shep sang it, looking like a curly-haired David Byrne, with Grace Abounds on keyboard, Bobby on bass guitar, Russ Never Sleeps on drums, and Molly, tiny and bouncy, chiming in on the harmonies. Now Molly works as a storyteller at parks and libraries, and Shep, having found his scholarly side, is finishing his mail-order Ph.D. in comparative religion.

■

"We were among the lucky ones," Shep reports. I follow his words as if they're stitches holding me together. "Your chimney has whiplash. The bricks are poking out like buck teeth. The big acacia fell. There's some broken glass, relics and icons. Some dishes. But otherwise, everything's fine. We're fine. Dove's fine. Everyone we know is fine."

I sigh with relief. I imagine I'm back there, on the deck on a moonless night when everything really was fine, the stars straining backward into the sky, the coyotes giggling and shrieking under the ponderosas as if they're turning themselves inside out.

The owl I used to hear every month or two has befriended Shep now that he's moved in, he's told me, swooping past with a noise like a skateboard racing down a hill. Whenever I call Shep, it hoots. "There it is," Shep says. "Listen."

Molly picks up the extension. "I was in the elevator in the library," she says, in the melodious voice children love to listen to. "I pressed the up button and the quake started. Talk about guilt. Dove was with me, thank God. You don't have to come up, everything's under control. All that day it was very still, like after a snowfall. But hot, scary. That uncanny waiting feeling, like it was perfecting what it was about to do."

When she stops talking I can hear threads of birdsong weaving through the air — the yellow warblers that arrived last year at this time and sat in the live oaks and the holly bush.

Molly puts Dove on. She's four. *A love,* Esther says.

"What did the earthquake sound like, sweetie?" I ask.

"It sounded like earthquake damage," she says in her clear trill.

"What's that like?"

"Crack crack crack. The giant was playing."

"The Giants, honey," Shep corrects.

"The giant hit the earth smack on the dot. It might have been the home plates inside."

"You know, this was a clone of the nineteen-oh-six quake in San Francisco," Shep says.

Three days of fire and a hundred thousand dead, Esther says. *The day I came through Ellis Island.*

"Molly's got her agoraphobia again. I haven't seen her like this since she was hit by lightning, and —"

"Lightning? Are you kidding?"

"Yeah," she says. "Three years ago. I thought if you had a child you should have an umbrella. So the electricity would come through the tip of my umbrella and go like a shimmer through my whole body. Everything was black and white like an old movie. This has called it all up. Is Dove off the phone? My therapist says, 'Which doesn't belong: being sick, being tired, being depressed, leaving the house.' But I say to her, 'Which doesn't belong: eating your breakfast, doing your shopping, picking up your daughter at the day-care center, having a building fall on you.'"

"We're okay, basically," Shep says soothingly. "We'll take care of things. Don't worry about anything."

When they get off the phone I sink into the sofa, numb.

They'll take care of things. "I've been hit by lightning, too," I say after a while into the dial tone. Esther is humming, her lips pressed together. *A home without a child,* she says, visible at that instant, looking around for what isn't there.

6

"Is it you I thank for my getting through?" I ask her.

Whatever you do, shayne madele, don't call yourself a survivor, because you never know.

"Superstition?"

Superstition is for the shtetl. She sniffs, a Litvak lift of her head. *It's a wail of tears,* she says with her Russian accent. *God says to us, you're a Jew, may you live heavily ever after. It's chutzpah to think you're exempt.*

"But you just told me about the czar —"

For now, for now. Look, think of my brother Boris, may he rest in peace, a mathematics professor, an orchestra conductor, so lucky to escape the Pale. He was brilliant, he got through the university where they ordinarily didn't allow Jews, then he was a professor of mathematics in beautiful St. Petersburg. So he starved to death in the siege of Leningrad. There was absolutely no food. Think of that! No food! They have half a million trees for people who died. On Nevsky Prospekt they keep the sign, still: CITIZENS, THIS SIDE OF THE STREET IS SAFEST IN CASE OF SHELLING. *People put flowers there, a branch of pine. He had red hair.*

"You were there?"

I know.

I knew, and I am able to imagine, with my genetic memory, the Old Mother, where you ate beets and onions and cabbages and, if you were better off, a boiled chicken and, if you were lucky and rich, an orange. It echoes down genetic memory lane, the terrifying pogroms and hunger, into the winter sun of Santa

Cruz that mimics the weather of Spain and Jerusalem. Heart is where the home is. I'm ravenous for roots. But what good are roots if the earth keeps moving?

7

I've been shaken loose. It's been a month since the earthquake, and still I trust nothing unless it's soft. Framed paintings, bibelots (*chatchkas,* Esther says), canned goods, heavy books, seem ready to detach from their moorings, ready to make a mistake. Any building could fall on me. I can't concentrate; I shiver in the warm, even temperatures. *Confusion is a form of grief,* a voice reminds me. Molly is oddly incommunicado, and Shep assures me that I needn't fly up, that everything is fine. Esther is with me always, worried about the fate of San Diego: *If they build over the deserts there will be no place for the prophets,* she frets. My longing for Santa Cruz is now like worry about a dying friend. Then a national magazine asks me to write an article about the aftermath, and I fly north to gather impressions.

8

Esther is looking around at the brooding mountains covered by leaded nets that keep the loosened earth from sliding onto the highway. *Fifteen years of your life here,* she says. *Our five-thousand-year-old hunger for trees.*

Bobby drives the deadly snaking road that connects Santa Cruz to the rest of the world. It's been a week since the anniversary of Kristallnacht, a week since the Berlin Wall has come down. His finely chiseled face looks sad and drawn. He has cut his long blond hair short as if to face the facts:

"There are ten thousand homeless people in the county. In

Watsonville there are tent cities, people camped in parks," he says in a strained voice. I remember the way the vista opens softly just before Watsonville. You can smell things growing there, things people like to eat. Acres of apple orchards, the heavy boughs supported by sticks, magnolia trees scattered among them.

"The earthquake knocked a million apples off the trees," Bobby says.

Windfall, a voice murmurs.

"So the wall has fallen," I say, as Pink Floyd, on the radio, plays the first chords of "The Wall." Bobby turns it up. "There's a kind of coincidence fever going on now," he says. "Everyone's seeing this net of connections where the old foundation has slipped away. It's true," he says, looking over at me, his light blue eyes wide. I'm never sure what he believes: He can go from gullible to charmingly cynical in seconds.

He cuts into the left lane and I hang on to my door. The forest leans in on both sides. We are spinning through deep woods.

"People say it relaxed the mountains, but I don't know, I feel the trees and they don't feel relaxed. I feel as if someone's dreaming us, someone who has no preferences. As if we are seriously useless. I'm kind of screaming inside all the time now. There's nothing wrong with going crazy. I'd rather do it fast, though, not a nervous breakdown like a wall falling in slow motion." With his hair cut, he looks bare and dematerialized, the last remnant of an evaporating flamboyance.

"Russ Never Sleeps is heading for New York; he says it's safer," Bobby continues in a hypnotic monotone. "But you know how Santa Cruz is. You get as far as Wisconsin and then you change your mind and come back." Bobby himself did this a couple of years before, driving east on the interstate, then turning around and driving west, then east for an hour, then west and back to the coast, calling up friends every time he changed direction.

He turns to me. "You can sense things moving here; when you

leave Santa Cruz it's like a hum has stopped. Even ten miles up the coast you don't hear it," he says. He gives a sad little laugh. "I felt sorry for you having to leave Santa Cruz but now it's gone for all of us. I even feel fond of the potholes of blissed-out ignorance I used to hate. Convictions can accumulate around anything here," he mutters, as the truck swings around a curve, a case of tools sliding about under my seat. "But," he says, taking another curve, "it's resonant. Maybe that's why we got shattered, like a wineglass. We'll be there in ten minutes. I thought I'd take you downtown later. So you see it for the first time in the dark."

Even now, out of the corner of my eye I notice a hill that's brown where the rubble tumbled down. I don't see the spire of the white Catholic church, and there's too much space on the hill where it used to sit. My heart drops. As we get closer I can feel that the city is fragile, a shell without viscera, like something you nudge with your toe on the sand.

Don't look, Esther says, as we head for the Casa Blanca near Main Beach where, a year before, lightning hit a woman and melted her bathing suit. There never used to be thunder and lightning here. Bobby is saying he's going to dye his hair green to advertise his landscaping business. Somewhere — he shrugs — they painted a bridge blue and people stopped jumping off it. It hardly seems the same, but I nod, saving my energy for the evening, eager for the sea. *Eager not to see,* a voice says redundantly.

9

I sit on the terrace of the Casa Blanca, drinking in the pale-tea-colored horizon that precedes sunset. The freshness of the air is astonishing, a world away from the stale drafts in my office in the Being and Nothingness Building at the university. There is some ingredient that enlarges the psyche here, the positioning of the mountains, the mating arrangements of land and water. A mile north, at Lighthouse Point, the surfers are poised inside the last waves of the day, waves that peel, as usual, in a perfect scroll. Above me a gull tilts origami wings, and a skein of long-beaked pelicans floats by, as if it's a banner that reads, GOING SOUTH. I think I hear the silent lurch and rattle of the Big Dipper, blocks away, but it's only on the weekends that the amusement park is a fairyland of stuttering neon, slender arcs of light in the pink dusk. You can feel the ghosts of the old amusements then, the Neptune Casino, the Electric Pleasure Pier. In World War II — *Ravensbrück, Auschwitz,* Esther whispers — the lights on the boardwalk were blocked out when canvas curtains were draped from the casino to the mouth of the river, the darkness a weapon against enemy aircraft. Now the golden bowl of the sun halves itself in the ocean and disappears from sight, as I eat apples and nuts, a meal for a small mammal. In the twilight I watch the mile buoy blinking every seven seconds. Then darkness descends, and a full moon wobbles, bibulous, on the waves. It's a warm evening. Mantilla inklings, nights in the gardens of Spain.

Until the Expulsion, Esther says.

10

The sight of it wipes the smile off my face. The promenade is rubble, block after block, a bombed-out zone. A few buildings still stand, out of kilter, as if a familiar face had undergone a stroke. Their souls are gone. Anyone can look in. Behind the yellow tape and chain-link fence it's flattened, open. The clouds in the new spaces are floating memorials, floating over the rubble, over the white stink of plaster dust you can still smell.

It's gone.

The Lost and Found Cafe is gone. The Good Times Building next to it is gone. The Trust Building, where Michael and I got our peaceful and agonizing divorce, is gone. There is no sound.

It's unearthly. It swarms with absences. I sit down on the sidewalk and rock back and forth. Esther is singing, "Who Will Know Me?" a song so sad it must be Russian.

Bobby crouches down and peers into my face in the dark. "Let's think of all the flowers we know the smells of," he says.

"Freesia," I say weakly.

"Gardenia."

"Freshly cut grass." I can barely speak.

He pulls me up and gets me to walk. Esther looks at the wreckage. *Like a Cossack in a sukkah,* she says. It feels as if evil spirits have been let loose in a feast of malice. After a few minutes we stop in front of a garden. Moonlight is part of the trees. I see two old rosebushes, the white flowers flat and open.

"I made this garden out of plants from collapsed houses," Bobby says.

The earth is a pensive thing. It thinks through its gardens, Esther murmurs, her voice an evening breeze in the dark.

Bobby and I sit down on two crates, velvety tibouchina leaves brushing like a spiderweb against my cheek. I think I can hear night bugs nibbling the orphaned flora. Bobby's tools — clippers, pruners, trowel, rake — are lying around in a reverie of work.

"You're catching up with our shock," he says hoarsely, his voice echoing from the bushes that are gray as gravestones in the night. "The bass note of life is that you're always waiting for something big to happen and now it has, but it isn't what we expected. Every time I'm downtown I freak out."

He breaks off a small branch of the tibouchina and I touch the scar of attachment left on the stem. His hand, when I reach for it, is clammy. I know how many of his friends have died, and now this.

He takes a small flashlight out of the pocket of his leather jacket and aims it at a green, mildewed book lying on the ground, an old Modern Library copy of the *Decameron*. Autumn's small deaths are all around us, waiting for spring.

The Black Plague, Esther says. *They blamed it on the Jews. They said the Jews poisoned the wells. These people were meshugeneh. They said the Jews baked cookies shaped like Christian boys. The rabbis say hand washing before and after meals with prayers, that's how so many Jews survived.*

Bobby opens to the pages a bookmark divides and reads aloud in theatrical tones, his voice caroming off the trees: "'Who can deliver us from this plague? . . . the death-dealing pestilence which, through the operation of the heavenly bodies or of our own iniquitous dealings, being sent down for our correction by the just wrath of God . . .'

"Gimme a break," he says, his voice cracking. He opens the book again and looks up, reciting a part he seems to know by heart: "All tended to a very barbarous conclusion, namely to shun and flee from the sick and all that pertained to them."

"Someone left this book here," he says. "I don't know why. To make me crazy, maybe."

"Everything's so ambiguous in a catastrophe," I say. "Try not to attribute meaning to anything. There are books all over the place, probably, from the bookstores that were destroyed."

"Everyone knows it's my garden. It makes you feel jinxed. It drains your mental resources," he says.

It's getting damp, and I stand up, keeping a grip on his hand. The soil under us is as spongy as brake failure. We start back to the car. The moon has a shroud. The stars are not in evidence. The landscape feels like a big lie. I imagine the wall of screaming sirens, the gaping openings where walls had been.

"The garden is a good idea," I say when he drops me off at the Casa Blanca, the moonlight striking the waves in pieces. "It shows faith in the future. Really," I say, looking at his dejected face, his cropped blond hair prematurely white in the moonlight.

It's Esther murmuring when I'm alone again in my bed. She begins a bedtime story about her fiftieth wedding anniversary with Grandpa in Miami in the blond air, the palm trees like tropical *spritzes* of green a child could paint, *Ocean upon a time,* a story that gets tumbled into a dream all too soon, a dream where buildings are flinging themselves off a blue cliff into the sea.

11

The next morning I drive to my house in my rented car, up into the mountains, my red spiral notebook on the seat beside me. Little slaps and zigzags of tar are shining where the road has buckled. Smoke whispers from metal chimneys as startling as steel teeth. I know this route so well, know the trembling shade of the redwoods that falls on Graham Hill Road as it descends into the evergreen-rimmed valley. The earth is still humming, stunned.

Brown horses with white noses graze and nuzzle the manzanita, pastureland cut by the Zayante fault where Miocene shale embraces Eocene sandstone. Deep below me rest the fossils of horses, sea cows, camels, sand dollars. *See no sea here.* Four miles under the dead heaviness of the earth the tectonic plates scrape and scrape until they snag and *We're dice on a game board,* a voice says. *Yes,* Esther says, breathing deeply of the clear Northern California air, *like the dice Haman threw to decide which day to destroy the Jews.*

12

Shep's VW bus in the driveway still has its ZAPPA FOR PRESIDENT bumper sticker and a new one: FATE CONTINUES BUT ON NO ACCOUNT ABANDON YOUR OWN INTENTIONS. Molly has put a mezuzah on the doorjamb and I pat a kiss onto it, little pieces of Deuteronomy encased in a gold scroll so that when

Molly and Shep run for the doorway The Lord Our God Is One is there, pieces of the ancient story.

Shep opens the door before I ring and comes out and puts his arms around me. He's wearing a bright red sweater and jeans, his feet bare. His dark hair is long and wild. I had forgotten that when he smiles there's noplace else you want to be. "I Feel the Earth Move Under My Feet" is blasting behind him, Carole King, my old record. I know exactly what her voice is going to do, so familiar. I've come to dread the familiar: It only exists in order to testify to its own fleetingness.

"Turn it off so I can listen for rumbles," Molly yells from the kitchen. She comes in and wraps me in a hug that feels like a grandmother's and she looks, in fact, like Esther, a rose with Shoshone cheekbones, black hair, eyes of a muted darkness that is almost gray. *You know who she reminds me of?* Shep puts his arm around both of us; he likes having more than one woman in the room. His mobile face has more lines in it than it did three months ago. I notice that some of the kitchen cabinets are taped closed.

Molly extends her left hand and flashes a ring, a plastic artichoke with a rhinestone in the center like a baby in a cabbage patch.

Aftershock. Meaning artichoke.

"We thought we'd wait till you got here to tell you." She runs to the mantelpiece and shows me a cluster of small dark leaves and red flowers that I recognize as sage from the bush at the back of the garden.

"We got married in the garden. This was my bouquet. We put up a *chuppah* and it was a *sukkah* too. It was nice. You could see the stars through the hole in the pine branches and the bay laurel. We ate out there. Bay leaves kept falling in our soup."

She looks flushed and happy and slightly shy. I remember my wedding canopy, the seven blessings the rabbi recited over us, the crunch of the glass Michael stepped on to say we were part of the fated community that had its temple crushed, twice, the tremors of that catastrophe like a text we read in our sleep.

Molly gives me the bouquet to hold. "Weird. The earthquake happened during Sukkoth, the holiday when we're supposed to live under a canopy for a week, to remind us of the forty years of wandering in the desert. Now people are living in tents," Molly says, absentmindedly picking up Dove's toys and collecting them in a big basket: Lego pieces, a teddy bear with sunglasses, a shiny green party hat.

"It hit on October seventeenth," Shep says, their voices overlapping for a second. "Seventeen days after the Jewish New Year, the year fifty-seven fifty, which, if you add it up is seventeen."

"So they're blaming it on the Jews," Molly says, laughing. Esther shakes her head and makes a small *tsk,* and a jingling. Earrings.

"Really," Shep says. "It's incredible. We had a seven point one on October seventeenth, which is seven point one backwards. So you've got a seven point one, seven plus one equals eight at five-oh-four, five plus four equals nine, which is 'eighty-nine, the year, and eight and nine are seventeen, which is the date it happened. Our number was up; we should have divined it."

A scholar of gematria, Esther says.

Molly stretches out her hand. "Shep gave me this watch, too. Dove loves it. He painted the face. It's five-oh-three. Then it's five-oh-three again. Then it's five-oh-three some more."

"There's no time like my present," Shep says, laughing, kissing Molly's wrist, as the owl gives a daytime hoot from the ponderosas. "There it is," he says.

"Sit. There's something else," Molly says, leading me to the sofa I left behind, now covered with a Navajo blanket.

"We didn't want to tell you over the phone; you were having such a hard time adjusting down there. Please don't worry. It was tiny, one centimeter. They just took out a little bit of my breast. They did surgery, then I had radiation, like zaps of lightning. It was just a tiny lump. The surgeon was from New York and when she told me my chances of dying under anesthesia were the same as my being hit by lightning Shep told her I had been hit by lightning and she said, 'No problem, I just won't perform your surgery under a tree.' She had me in stitches."

I involuntarily look at her breasts, which look *zaftig,* as always, under her tight sweater with threads of Lycra-lightning woven through the wool. Two gray kittens I haven't seen before come into the room and purr around my ankles. "Shep got them for Dove when I was sick," Molly says, "to give her something else to think about."

"She named them both Bravery," Shep says.

Stay close to her, Esther urges.

"I was afraid the earthquake would pull the stitches out," Molly says. "The earth kept moving for the longest time. All this breast cancer shows our closeness to mother earth. When the earth is sick, people are sick."

"Was Grace any help?" I smooth Molly's arm. Grace had gone through worse three years before.

"Yes, as much as she could. But she's been a recluse, even more than I was. She went into retreat after they began demolishing buildings. I'm okay. I'll be fine."

"You look fine."

"And the house?"

"Things look fine here too," I say, although I notice that there are no crystals anywhere, and that makes me uneasy. In their last house there were crystals all over the place, slicing and dicing light, winking like a Busby Berkeley musical. A lot of things I've never even seen feel as if they're missing.

"So," Molly says, taking the glass of carrot juice Shep has brought to her, swishing the juice around in her mouth and swallowing. "We can change the subject. The wall is down. In Germany."

Injure many.

"They should have kept the wall," I say, "and put all the names from the Holocaust on it — Max Jacob, Bruno Schultz, Kafka's sisters —"

It would be longer than the Great Wall of China, Esther says. *To an American, six million sounds like nothing, but it was almost everyone.*

"A new Germany scares Molly," Shep says, "but I tell her it's not going to be like nineteen forty-two. And not here. And anyway" — he turns to her — "you don't look Jewish."

Molly bristles, Esther too. "That's not the point. And it's not a compliment."

"Hey, I wish I were Jewish," Shep says. "Christians are always imagining the wounds. I really like the warmth, and the law, and Kabbalah. When I think of culture I think of what's right in front of me, but you think of five thousand years."

"Everyone wants to be Jewish when it's the hora and Kabbalah but comes the pogroms and the Holocaust everyone's out the door," I say.

"Oh, Shep knows that," Molly says, patting his cheek. "He's been to twenty-seven bar mitzvahs. And you know his dissertation is on Kabbalah. And he helped me make the chicken soup," she calls as she goes into the kitchen.

It's the kitchen where Michael and I cooked 3,000 dinners together — gingered swordfish, *rogan josh,* bonbon chicken, lots of brown rice. But home is kugel, stuffed cabbage, blintzes, borscht, chopped liver, brisket, mushroom barley soup. What were we thinking of? The day after Michael left, Molly made me enough chicken soup to last a month.

Molly and Shep bring in three brimming bowls, golden broth, lengths of carrot, snowflake-light matzoh balls, and set them down on the white damask cloth, a wedding gift from Michael's aunt. My soup is in Dove's Miss Piggy bowl.

The same soul as mine, Esther says. *I also used to make for your uncle and father when they were small some apple pie with slivers of apricot and egg creams with three-cent bottles of seltzer and some fruit syrup, homemade.*

"I've been hearing my grandmother's voice," I say.

"After disasters ancestors show up at the thresholds." Shep nods.

"Our grandmothers were so solid," Molly says. "I really miss mine. The candles in brass candlesticks, the white tablecloth on Friday night. Compared to them we're just — holograms."

"My grandmother put a white cloth on the table every Friday night," Shep says.

"You never told me that." Molly looks at him. He's conducting with a soupspoon — "Whole Lotta Shakin' Goin' On." Does he listen to these records every day?

"My great-uncle Boris was a conductor," I say. "He had red hair."

"Red hair?" Molly says. We finish our soup and she seems a little dazed as we take the dishes into the kitchen. "Sit, be a guest. Red hair? Sit on the sofa. Shep will tell you all about the earthquake. Go, sit." She must still be tired from the weeks of radiation. "Tell her, Shep. I have to wake Dove up from her nap."

Shep sits next to me on the sofa and leans forward solicitously like a doctor with news. I open my notebook.

"My brother went into Ford's — the huge space where it had been — right after it happened, and there were people trying to drag a woman out of the debris so he intervened — he's a paramedic, remember — and this guy says, 'Get the fuck off! She's mine!' You're supposed to take the rocks off, first, when you're saving someone."

He lies down on the floor and puts his feet up on the cushion next to me. One of the kittens jumps onto his chest. "So I'll tell you what happened to me. I was downtown. I'd just finished at the chiropractor. I thought I was having some kind of bioenergetic energy surge. Then I realized. I ran to the doorway and the building collapsed behind me." He shuddered. "The whole building. There was a woman screaming that she had to get in there to get her wedding dress. It was terrible. You could hear glass shattering, gas hissing from the pipes, people yelling. The liquor store reeked of alcohol. Water was gushing out of second-story windows. Light poles whipped back and forth like fishing rods. Trees were falling everywhere. You could smell the woody pulp, pieces of the true cross. You wouldn't believe the thickness of the dust. Then everything was down."

I think of San Diego, the Sins of the Fathers library at the university, built on Jell-O landfill. In fifteen seconds geography can become history, shimmy of soft soil, absence of bedrock.

"It's incredible that I didn't break an ankle. The jumble of bricks was three feet deep. I was in shock. Chunks of brick were crashing down through skylights, tons of wood and brick were falling. There was a huge hole in the roof of Ford's." When I think of Ford's I remember a lacy pageant of lingerie; an unlikely source of the delicate and sexy silks Michael liked, this quiet old department store.

"The next thing I remember is police with police dogs sweeping through piles of brick to see if people were trapped underneath. I got to the other end of the mall, somehow. You couldn't breathe because you might set off the buildings. The bookstore had collapsed and there was a terrible white cloud of dust rising from the Coffee Roasting Company. And someone was saying, 'She is surely dead, the dogs can smell her,' and they were right. You remember her. Robin. She worked behind the counter, grinding coffee. Then it was dark and they couldn't search because if they ran the generator to give them light it would make too much vibration in the walls. Her friends went wild when they realized the police wouldn't search. The police clubbed them and put choke holds on them.

"It was more sheer force than you can possibly imagine. Molly made it back to the house and then her aunt got through from Michigan and told her now how serious the earthquake was and held the phone to the TV so Molly could listen to how the downtown ten miles away was falling to pieces. Like she hasn't been through enough lately. Molly was sure I was dead."

Suddenly I hear the sound of a chain saw and I open the sliding glass doors to the garden. I haven't written anything down. How would I have found Michael, if this had happened then? "They've finally come," Shep says. "We've been waiting for weeks."

Outside, a burly man is slicing into the fallen acacia, the chain saw's growl thick enough to split the earth. He seems dangerously close to the crabapple tree Michael and I planted eight years ago, a gesture of permanence undermined by our freelance lives. In September the apples are so ripe and sweet you can eat them from the tree, juicy chunks breaking off like pieces in a puzzle. I can't go out there — the garden is too potent.

"I didn't mean to be insulting before," Shep says. "You know that I know a lot about Jews. I learned from my alchemy studies that the Christians let the Jews be the gold merchants because gold was precious and the Jews were trusted. Molly thinks that when a disaster like this happens it's because we owe something to the world and we're sleeping through our debt. It's like moral insomnia. She thinks we weren't treating the homeless right and now a lot of people know what it's like to be homeless. She takes it too personally in some way. But in an earthquake you're not getting hurt because anyone hates you."

"That's the good side of it," I say. "The bad side is that you can't beg for mercy."

I think I hear Esther's voice, in an odd singsong, but it's Dove in the next room, reciting "Humpty Dumpty sat on a wall" in an obsessive incantation. Molly is trying to tell her a different story.

Shep clicks on the TV set and turns the sound all the way down. "Molly's doing really well now; she's strong, like Gracie was. The town is in bad shape though. It's not strictly realistic: It's autistic. The earthquake has made a big split between right and left brain. No one can talk straight and everyone's saying the same thing and everyone's talking way too much. A lot of voices got loose. The whole town is in my head. The voices have to go somewhere. Molly's telling everyone's stories at the library. The kids love her. Everyone wants to know where everyone else is. You want to keep track, just in case time and place get separated." His leg jiggles as he speaks.

I stare at the silent television set. A woman is doing her laundry, admiring a white tablecloth. I see Esther washing clothes in a big tub of hot water on top of the stove, in 1917 or so, washing the *hamantachen* costumes so the twins can be in the Purim play. Her story.

"I'm doing healings every Saturday afternoon," Shep says, "whoever wanders by. Some soul restoring. I know so many people in this town. They think I'm an authority on the sacred, now that I'm getting a degree. I'm working hard to bring about a change that will happen anyway. Come downtown tomorrow, you'll probably feel better. I'm sure a few people will show up."

Esther hears "show up" as *Shoah,* as she stands in the doorway with Molly, who's holding Dove in her arms, Dove dangling a Raggedy Andy doll with a face rubbed bare from loving.

"Let me ask four questions," Molly says, easing Dove down. "Was your grandmother named Esther, was your grandfather named Joseph, was she from Vilna, did she have twins?"

I nod, holding Dove, who has scrambled onto my lap. If Michael and I had stayed together, we might have had a child who looked like her, if we hadn't decided not to have a child.

"This blows my mind," Molly says. "This is too much." She begins to cry, leftover earthquake tears, people crying at the drop of a hat.

"I called my aunt. She'd mentioned Boris once, when I was in the band; he was a violinist, with red hair. Our grandmothers were sisters. They were barely in touch after my grandmother moved to Michigan. Your family didn't like my grandfather. We're second cousins." And she throws her arms around me.

Leah, Esther says. *Also Sophie, Cecile, Beatrice. Too poor for middle names.* Her sisters, some close and some scattered. I can see Esther now; she's in the room, her wavy hair swept back with two tortoiseshell combs. Her presence makes the news seem natural, almost expected. Of course Molly and I became friends.

"My aunt remembers you," Molly continues. "We visited you when I was three and you were four. We were bad. We went under the beds and came out covered with fluff. You were supposed to know better."

Shep laughs, a delighted giggle, and pats us on our backs as if we are two contestants who have won something. "You do have the same hair. Dove, too," he says as Dove runs and gets her Humpty Dumpty book to show me.

"I can't believe it," Molly and I are saying a hundred times. Then we laugh and say it again.

"You should get out those pictures," Shep says, and Molly comes back in a minute with a shoe box stuffed with snapshots and sets it on the kilim rug I left behind. *She's so much like me it isn't funny,* Esther says.

"There are people in here I can't identify," Molly says as she spreads the photographs out like a tablecloth.

There, Esther says. And there she is, looking both seductive and forthright. She wears a shirtwaist with jabot and frilly collar, her wavy black hair parted in the center. The thick grainy paper is sepia toned; 1905 is written on the back in watery brown ink. I stare at it, drinking in the shadows, the wedges and globes of light. She seems to glow, but then the whole picture glows — hall table, runner of lace. I feel sickened with recognition, as if I'm inhaling a volume of intimacy too large for my body.

Molly pulls another snapshot from the pile. In this one Esther holds a white rose and wears a Gibson girl blouse with a brooch at the neck and a straw skimmer. *Don't think I wore babushkas,* she says. Boris is seated next to her, a students' cap on his head, a stylish cane across his knee. Wallpaper flowers. Music falters in the background. It's a postcard and on the back is a Vilna address, half obliterated. My eyes wink and twitch and sparkle with too much energy.

Then there is Esther in a cloth coat with a beaver collar, Esther in a flowered dress, in the New World's air and light, fewer people in the world then, air you could breathe. Fort Tryon Park, Morris Avenue in the Bronx, Sylvan Lake, Mt. Eden, Mt. Freedom, places I've never been, places that hold still.

Ordinary places, Esther says. I see her lowering a thick record onto the turntable of the tall Victrola. *Melba, Gluck, Galli-Curci.* Her fragrance is like challah, sweet and eggy.

They turned the Jews into bread, the voice says, not hers, and then corrects itself, *into soup. Into soap.*

She sits at a piano. *You have to play Schubert as if you know a secret,* she says.

We keep finding photographs. Leah and Esther arm in arm, looking soft and generous. "You're too used to kindness," Michael used to say to me. "Your family didn't prepare you for the world."

After a while the sun falls somewhere; the chain saw is silent. Shep goes out to pick up a pizza, and Molly lights two candles as the sky turns dark. We watch the flames shiver into narrowness and widen again as we sit in silence, Dove between us teaching

Raggedy Andy to read Humpty Dumpty. Then Shep comes back, balancing the box on two fingers; Esther sniffs the pepperoni, turns her head away. *Take a sourball,* she says. I imagine a lemon one the same size as the marbles in the Chinese checkers she let me win at, each in its hole on the board patterned in a Star of David design.

It grows late, the candles burned down to splashes of white wax, and I anticipate the drive back to the ocean through the redwoods and ponderosas with their night moisture, their fragrant relief at being left alone by the sun, the animals among them nocturnal and alert or curled up in sleep. I can already smell the damp debris of redwood needles, the fog quenching the thirst of the evening.

In Nemincinya Forest, in the forest of Ponary, on the outskirts of Vilna, tens of thousands vanished, shot and thrown into graves the Germans forced them to dig themselves. To dig your own grave takes time. Her forests.

At the door Molly gives me a crystal. "I put them away because of the radiation," she says. "Too much light."

Don't keep it near your bed, Esther urges me.

"Don't keep it near your bed," Molly says. "If there's an earthquake it could put out your eye."

13

A dream fallen into the night must be retrieved.

A dream that is not understood is an unopened letter from God, Esther says.

That night I dream I'm in a struggle with Esther: We are Jacob and the angel. Her wings flutter like the veils of a tropical fish. *Jacob and the angel did not mean problem,* she says. *People were still mud then, still being made. He was taking the impression of the angel.*

Then she's stamping snow off her galoshes and I am hugging her, sometime in the 1940s. I smell the fresh cold in the wool of her coat, forming me.

14

Dawn is tender above the untouched mountains and the bay is a deep blue, waking from its Sabbath sleep. It's Saturday, the Sabbath, when according to tradition we are loaned an additional soul, a rose without thorns. Two souls, one ghost, many voices, an unexpected cousin. Too much.

As I slide a sweater over my head Esther chides, *Don't wear black so much, you won't remember your childhood,* so I change to a green blouse — to match Bobby's hair. Then we walk toward the amusement park, the citrus slice of the Ferris wheel motionless in the morning light that holds every object as succinctly as a catcher's mitt cradling a ball.

I sit on the wooden steps of the boardwalk and look at my palm, lines of lineage and divination, my life. *Tests passed smashed, earrings you had mentioned, the wedding jewels,* a voice says. Shockley's. My absent wedding ring no longer a white strip on my finger. We split up, reluctant but in agreement about the necessity, at the Trust Building, now a shambles, signed the papers in an office on the second floor. *Seaweed askew, whose house is this:* a different voice. Esther is silent now but I can see her: She dunks a little in the sea, scooping handfuls of water onto her arms and face, her one-piece bathing suit sopping. When I was two she rode the waves with me in her arms, buoying me gently as if she were lifting me high above a parade I had to see.

Now, as then, the breakers darken, sparkle at the rim, and crash into foam.

Don't dwell on faults, says Swami Beyondananda, Esther halloos from beyond the waves.

15

A few minutes later I'm downtown, listening to Canned Heat on KUSP and doing a parking space visualization, which, I suddenly realize, is pointless: Nothing is where it used to be. I look in vain for the street that leads from the pier, and take the long way around past the big permanent tents the city has put up. Hammering noises come from houses on the next block, houses that still tilt at the angle of the earth's tantrum.

Booktent Santa Cruz is arranged exactly as it was when it was the bookshop, section by section, aisle by aisle. I get lost in Neruda's *Residencia en la Tierra* and, as I walk out, drenched in Spanish, *the language that laps at our southern borders like a tranquil sea,* a voice reminds me, I notice the floor under my feet. It's a thin plank of wood over space. It's nothing. *It's not a floor,* the voice whispers.

But the post office is intact, with its old WPA murals of men handpicking artichokes and strawberries in lush fields. You can see them in their baseball caps and pesticide veils, scarves around their necks, on the drive down to now-ruined Watsonville, killing their backs and knees at $3.65 an hour, the acid strawberry juice running into the cuts in their hands, their figures small in the green distance.

Across from the post office, the side of a building reads, DANGER WALL MAY FALL KEEP AWAY. In Berlin, people have been grabbing pieces of the fallen wall as souvenirs. *Berlin,* Esther says. *It was silent except for the sound of stained glass breaking in all the synagogues, on Kristallnacht. We were here. Every single synagogue in Germany. Frieda, my friend, may she rest in peace, arrested later by the SS, complained to the police about the smashed windows in her store and they just laughed at her.*

I can feel her fretfulness. How can I love my safety enough?

"Where we are now is just a river basin hemmed in by faults, that's all," I say, "A town built on a floodplain next to a fault line. That's all it is. It has nothing to do with anything."

Like I'm standing on the ceiling it doesn't, she says. *Wait till you're old enough.*

16

I've stopped in front of the post office to marvel at the clarity of the late-morning light when I see a half-familiar figure ambling up. It's Grace, slender and pretty, her blonde hair now as short as Bobby's and heavily threaded with gray. She was a girl from good eastern schools when she came to Santa Cruz, an American who has never had to know about inner crossings back and forth to the Old Country. She has spent years undoing her perfections, and today she is doing it with almost black lipstick, and a powdered pallor.

She plants a kiss on my cheek. "I was just picking up my mail, on my way to meet you and Molly. So you're cousins — amazing. Gossip spreads like wildfire now."

Wildflowers.

She reaches for a leathery datura blossom on the bush next to me and tucks the yellow bloom into my hair. "It's great to have you back. I haven't been down here in so long," she says, putting her arm through mine.

She quickens her step, almost panicky, as we pass a dizzying gap in the landscape: The Cooper House — with its art galleries, flower shops, cafe, mahogany bar, one of the oldest buildings — is missing. We had all listened to jazz there, sipping our Calistogas on the terrace, peace spread out before us as we gazed at the sidewalk strollers passing by. Civilized. Like 1912. A huge stained-glass canopy where the jazz trios played. It was the center of the center.

"I can't remember what it looked like," I say anxiously.

"Yellow brick like the road in *The Wizard of Oz*. It got through the 1906 quake but they destroyed it with the wrecking ball nine days after this one, no one knows why. A big crowd was watching and we all held our breath. Then they bashed it in. The last thing I noticed before it came down was FOREVER JOY written on the lintel. Some people got used to seeing the dust rise and settle but I stayed away after that," she says in the low husky voice that Bobby envies and loves to imitate. "A blonde who makes dark sounds," Shep used to say when she sang backup with the band.

We keep walking, and Grace points to a lamppost where Xeroxed photos of lost cats and dogs loom like ghosts. "People are Xeroxing like mad," she says. "The urge to reproduce. They dream about babies. Even me."

I write that down in my notebook, along with "bashed it in," leaning on Grace's back.

When we reach the huge wooden fence that cuts off the many blocks of damage from pedestrian traffic, I see that the fence is covered with language, pages and pages of poems stapled neatly in long rows across its expanse — Poets-in-the-Schools, Creative Elders. The one nearest me reads:

> *The day wheeled to a dot. The heavens seized.*
> *Concisest of catastrophes.*

Like Emily Dickinson, Esther says. *I used to read her in Yiddish. Such a language of compression. I read Shakespeare, Dickens.*

Grace stares at the poems, her mind clearly elsewhere. I turn to another one:

> *Thud of utter dread*
> *and the flying around.*
> *Strangers you may have to get to know quickly.*
> *I lived through many, the earth shaking my teeth.*

I lived through it. I didn't want to,
but I lived through it.

"Amen," says Grace, tightening her grip on my arm.

17

A filtered light from wide windows falls on the pink tablecloths
and green carpet at India Joze, everyone's favorite restaurant,
which is unharmed only a block from the collapsed buildings.
The pinks and greens are Polo Lounge colors; movie stars sat
among these same hues at the Beverly Hills Hotel in the fan magazines I read as a child. A mile away was Romanoff's, which belonged to the faux prince who was Boris's brother-in-law, from
the Old Country, the one who stole a name from his oppressors,
the one who made good.

At Romanoff's, where the stars ate, they had lemons in gauze,
like the citron you imagine at the center of your heart during Jewish
meditation, so it wouldn't squirt. Like the wedding glass wrapped
in paper so the shards wouldn't fly into our eyes when Michael
crushed it underfoot.

"I'm so glad I wasn't on the road when it happened," Grace
says, throwing her light shawl over the back of her chair, as we sit
down across from Molly. "Some guy was driving home on Route
1 — remember, Molly? — and three horses ran out from the
farmlands toward the ocean, scared to death, and slammed into
him and he died."

Shuddered, screamed, bolting, foaming, Esther says. *Cossacks*
with swords on horses. We would lock up the house as if no one lived
there, we would hide in the cellar. Then no one did live there. We
came to America.

I open my notebook as Molly beckons the waiter. "The downtown?" Grace says, smoothing the flat half of the front of her

black T-shirt with white letters that say BODIES FREE BEACHES. "I think of it as, aliens came and lifted it up and took it some-where. I believe it's elsewhere." She pats Molly on the shoulder. "Sorry, I don't mean to be so dramatic. You still need to rest."

She turns to me. "You can write this down. I was about to go trim the goats, topless as usual. Then I saw the tsunami in the hot tub just as I was thrown to the ground. A tornado comes whirling down the road and there's time to hide. A hurricane has an eye. But an earthquake is like vomiting: Suddenly everything gets lost and rearranged. There's a thing you're ripe for when it all gets taken away, but what is it?"

A huge passing truck shakes the building and Grace jumps, pale as a ghost. "I don't believe this is happening again. It just never ends. We're being thrown off the earth," she says in a high, unfamiliar voice, she who has been so brave, she who had a Tree of Life tattooed on her chest three years before. There's a famous picture of her, arms flung wide, naked, one breast missing, her head thrown back in celebration of life, a beautiful blonde. She distributed the photograph in her campaign to get the laws changed for Santa Cruz beaches: With air on our breasts, she'd argued, we'd have no cancer there.

She runs her hand through her punk cut as if she still expects to find her fairy-princess-no-harm-shall-befall-me hair. "You get extremely anxious. You learn to become very sensitive to your furniture. And the weather. Today I'm real edgy because the weather is beautiful."

It *is* beautiful. And unseasonably hot, which is bad. Even in town you can sense the hawks on the ridge lifts, the brilliant sky rinsing everything, pouring down what could turn out to be a spiteful quiet.

The waiter, who knows us, brings the samosas we always used to order, and I realize I haven't had breakfast; I'm starving.

This is not starving, Esther chides. *Boris starved to death, so thin and shrunken they folded him up into a baby carriage, his red hair like the color of a pine tree when it's sick. They wheeled him to the concert hall. His skin was parchment, but he could listen. And Romanoff on this side of the water had such a famous restaurant, such a beautiful restaurant.*

A minor tremor shakes the room and panic pulls at my stomach. The three of us reach for each other's hands.

"Do you believe in God?" Grace turns to Molly. I know they've been through this before but she wants a distraction.

Molly nods. "You know I do, Gracie."

"I believe in God when my plane lands," Grace says, fingering the rosary of string-of-hearts leaves that spills from the planter above our table.

Molly laughs. "That's a start."

"Well, you have a child," Grace says, as if that explains everything.

"Oh," Molly says, "that reminds me." She fishes a deckle-edged snapshot from her purse. "I found another photo. It couldn't be anyone but you."

We look at my chestnut braids and pinafore. I'm four, dangling a vine of plump tomatoes from the Victory Garden. *Such a sweet face,* Esther says.

"You can have it," Molly says, as a second tremor wobbles our table.

"Is the Messiah coming?" Grace breathes. "All these catastrophes." It's true: In Santa Cruz alone there have been floods, mudslides, forest fires, dozens of people evacuated from their houses forever. In Hawaii Pele is pouring molten lava over villages, pitting the windows of jet planes with plumes of ash. Then there are Lyme ticks, the sinking water table, falling meteors.

The Messiah is evanescent, Esther whispers. *He and She have come and gone a million times, and I don't mean false ones. But your grandfather used to say, You do not wait for the Messiah, the Messiah waits for you.*

At that moment a woman with a chalky face and red lips that look like the wax lips we clamped to our mouths when we were children wanders into the restaurant. Her black hair is bunched and witchy; it stumbles all over her head.

"God loves you!" she shouts to everyone, as seven tables of people look up at her.

Grace turns to me, her blue eyes full of pity. "People are detoxing all over the place. I've seen her around. Everyone's either sick or a healer these days, or both. Even me. I'm studying craniosacral work. You adjust the cranial plates and it changes the rhythm of the fluid in the brain. The physical is political." She puts her hand on top of my head and after a minute it feels like rain.

The woman is almost at our table now, the waiter nervously hurrying toward her. "God loves you!" she cries in a haunted voice. "God loves you!" Then she is keening over the photo of me and the tomatoes, swaying forward and backward. "God loves you! Strange! Upset! You ate tomatoes!" People at the other tables look both dismayed and accepting.

"It could be anyone," Molly explains softly. "Hardly anything happens to only one person anymore."

Grace puts a hand on the woman's shoulder. Her hands look smaller than they did on the keyboard, as if they have grown shy. "It's okay," she says to her. "It's okay." She wraps a samosa in a napkin and stuffs it into the woman's coat pocket. Then she guides her gently toward the door, her hand steady on the woman's back.

"She's not the Messiah," I say to Molly, scribbling a doodle in my notebook as lonely as a line on a seismograph. "She's just a coincidence."

"Maybe coincidences are angels," Molly says. "Shep is always saying that god is chance." She pokes at the petals of a gold chrysanthemum in a vase on the table. "It's a relief to talk to you, you know how it's not hip to be Jewish in Santa Cruz. People who come to places to shed identities and be transformed don't like to be reminded of the past, and we can't help it, we carry history around with us, it breaks into every minute of our lives. Actually, I would never be able to stand the certainty of a Messiah who's already arrived." She sniffs the flower and sets the vase in front of Grace's plate.

Grace comes back and sits down. "I did some work on her spine," she says.

I can see the woman through the window; she's sitting on a stone bench in the midst of the yellow rosebushes and white-flowered shepherd's needle. She nibbles into her napkin and we all watch her. How did she become this? How do we lose our marbles in life's Chinese checkers? When she finishes eating she lifts her head so that her lips, still vermilion, seem to float in thin air.

"God loves you!" she howls, inflecting the vowel oddly, histrionically, this time, so that it sounds like "God starves you!"

I cover my ears to keep my heart from concurring. Molly's soft round face and Grace's patrician features wear the same look of weary concern.

Poor thing, Esther says. *He didn't live through it. He wanted to, but he didn't.*

18

Shep is stationed across from DANGER WALL MAY FALL in an empty lot combed clean of rubble, half a block from Bobby's garden. He looks like a figure of power in his white linen dashiki, its sleeves and collar trimmed with beads and cowrie shells.

A few people have gathered, but he's waiting — *for a minyan,* Esther whispers — and he takes up a small drum with a hole in the center, like a Purim drum, and pushes and pulls an abbreviated broom handle in and out, making a gaspy sound. After several minutes he starts speaking quietly, looking directly into the eyes of the ten people collected there. They gaze at him with rapt attention.

"Santa Cruztaceans, I'm not here for you to say, 'Whoa, it's a miracle, I'm healed,' or 'My prosperity problems have disappeared.' I just want you to tell us what happened. I want you to be the Scheherazades of smithereens. We're a tortoiseshell the diviners held over the fire until we cracked, and now we read the lines of fracture, which are our stories." I can see he's a little nervous, an old shyness turned inside out, like in the days of the band.

A woman steps forward without hesitation, a woman I used to see on the mall, another lost-marbles case, whose constant companion was a mangy Irish setter. "My scars are changing places," she mumbles, bending over to comb her dog's tangled hair with a stick.

"Okay, good, that's a beginning." Shep smiles at her patiently.

"Bottom line, he doesn't like to see anyone hurt," Molly used to say about him, even in the years when he was fused to the glitter of his local rock-star status. When Michael and I parted, Shep took me to the movies four days in a row, matinees that left me mercifully blinded when I stepped out into the street.

"It's a knife in your life," a gravelly voice mutters, a homeless man who came to a gallery opening last year. He digs into a soiled carton of chow mein with a white plastic spoon.

"It crippled my soul," a lanky man with long hair joins in. "I couldn't stop screaming when I ran out of my apartment."

"The earth is having major major boundary problems," calls a woman walking by, making a megaphone with her cupped hands.

"I was doing work on a house," says a slender vegetarian-looking young man. "On a scaffold, and I saw street after street begin to move, from up high, a wave traveling through the whole city."

Libidinous. Some voice.

"I was out in the waves, surfing," a woman with streaked blond hair announces, "and I saw the cliffs rippling and then slipping down."

"I got out of my car to check my tires," a woman in jeans, no bra, attractive at fifty, says. "Then I saw twenty other people who'd gotten out of their cars to check their tires and then I knew what it was."

"The leaves on the trees were rattling like a death rattle," a man with glasses mumbles.

"Last week in Vermont," Grace says, "I finally got away and I was walking in the woods and it was as if something was missing — the fear in my body. I still dream of houses lurching into flames, becoming turnstiles of flame," she says huskily, running a hand over her cropped hair.

"Panic comes when you know what necessity is," says the homeless man, trying to tear open a packet of catsup. "It gets you, inside. I get a choking feeling when I eat. Sometimes I walk and walk."

"No one sleeps naked anymore," Molly says, looking sad. "All I want is to sleep in the darkness in nothing but skin."

Shep waits to see if anyone else wants to speak. We are all silent, standing closer together than before. Then he takes a breath several sentences long and lifts his arms as if inviting more light to this small plot of dirt that sits over river silt. His brown hair curls at the neck of the white dashiki. He extends his arms.

"Now, close your eyes. Focus on your breath, on your breathing rhythms. Breathe deeply. Slowly. Think of yourself as a hollow channel vibrating with energy. Let a waterfall of light and breath stream through your body. Slowly. The Kabbalists call this 'The House Is Being Built.'"

I open my eyes a little and see them all with eyes closed, expressions of concentration on their faces. They believe in him; they are hungry for wholeness. Although the scar lady mutters, "What is *this?* Simon Says?"

I close my eyes and breathe deeply, for the first time in weeks, months. The air is so clear I can breathe all the way in, one breath connected to the other. I remember Esther crocheting an afghan, with stitches that looked like grains of cooked barley, the ivory crochet hook grabbing the next stitch and the next, inclusive, friendly. My whole body is vibrating with fine tremors.

I feel Shep moving among us, touching everyone. His hand rests for a brief instant on my shoulder, and then he says to us, "Open your eyes, slowly, gently. Notice how you're all breathing in the same rhythm. Things want to pulse in coincidence. Like fireflies." I open my eyes slowly and see everyone else blinking, eyes shining.

You do not wear out time when you talk to God, Esther says. Then, in a warm voice, *There's Dove.* Bobby's truck is at the curb and he is lifting a delighted Dove from the front seat — her legs in blue overalls bicycling in the air — and hoisting a small red folding chair in his other hand. His hair is only partly green, a metallic blondness peeking out here and there.

"My daughter." Shep grins at us, waiting, as Bobby settles Dove in her chair. Then Shep unties the yellow tie from a green plastic garden bag and he and Molly pull out a profusion of white silk and spread it on the ground. It looks like a huge tablecloth, not yet set for the rituals. I see that it's the parachute Molly sometimes uses when she tells stories in the park.

We all stand there in the stillness of the warm day. Shep, looking cheerful, cheeks flushed, bends his knees and straightens them.

"This is the motion," he says. "Now everyone take a section of the parachute, and bend and straighten your knees, bend and straighten. Don't forget to breathe." Molly, next to him, bends and straightens her knees, gently, looking powerful beyond her smallness, her long paisley skirt belling out. *She'll be fine,* Esther says.

We each lift our portion of the white silk and flap it once, then billow it up and down, inhaling and exhaling, our exhalations sounding like the sighing that moves through treetops. Soft, silken thin, the parachute collects the wind and makes a deep hollow *whupping,* beating like a slow heart as we move it up and down, inhaling and exhaling. I can see the chicken-wire pattern in the translucent silk, extremely beautiful with the sunlight coming through. As the parachute billows it becomes a dome, with a hole at the top that allows a glimpse of the sun.

Like a sukkah, Esther says.

"Aaah men," Shep breathes. He and Molly lower their portion of the parachute carefully and we follow suit. Pointillist dots dance in my visual field.

Shep bows his head. He puts his hands on his lower abdomen and sways forward and back, slowly at first, then with more force. "Thank you, you who have kept us alive and sustained us and permitted us to remain," he intones in a baritone deeper than usual. He lifts his head and rocks back and forth on his heels, chanting melodically in a cantorial voice, his face flushed. I wonder what this takes out of him: After a Missing Children performance he used to sleep for two days.

"If you are rock, look at me," he chants in a minor key, and we murmur, after, like voices in an Orthodox shul. *If you are rock, look at me.*

"If you are water, look at me." His words evaporate into our echo: *If you are water, look at me.*

"If you are sky, look at me."

If you are sky, look at me, we respond.

Holy, holy, holy, Esther says. *He's davening, saying Kaddish for Santa Cruz.* He does look like a rabbi at this moment, with his aquiline nose and his rough brown curls. We have formed a circle around him, swaying forward and back, in the trance of his energy.

"Meet water," he chants, making a wavy gesture with his hand. Dove waves back from her chair. My body feels like water, a river of energy.

"Meet earth." He drums hard on the ground with his feet, like a flamenco dancer, and we stamp ours in the same rhythm, timidly, afraid to tempt the earth.

"Meet fire!" he shouts, and runs, fast, around the perimeter of our group, first one way, then the other, his dashiki ballooning out behind him. He is someone else now, familiar and unfamiliar. The Irish setter is barking. I can feel a delta wave of deep meditation building up in me as Shep encircles us. My listening is sensitive as an insect's: Our clothes rustle and shift on our bodies. Under me, the earth, rich and warm, sends tremors. The afternoon shadows are stretched thin.

"Meet air," Shep says loudly, panting. He is in place now, his hair wild, his face ruddy. He raises his hands as if to bless us. "This," he says in a soft voice, "is how one person is transformed into the entire creation." And at the word *creation* I hear the voice of the earthquake, a rumbling, a roaring, whose shaking turns into a fierce trembling in my tired body that I can't control. I see Molly look at me, startled, as if she has seen a bolt of lightning, just as a powerful current zings up my spine and surges through me with great velocity. I've never left my body before. As I depart I hear Michael's voice saying, *Take your keys.*

19

Out of the blue I am in the troposphere, riding my second soul into the blue, high above the crowd, all their heads like seedpods far below. The redwood forests are a heavenly green softness.

The surf crackles its silver brocade in silence, all lace and shimmer. I can no longer hear the waves wallop and sigh in their ancient roar of commiseration. The face of the reservoir looks terrified: Water must have a memory. The ozone layer, the planet's caul, is tearing and thinning.

I don't mind flying, Esther says, soaring next to me, a Chagall mirage, an airborne mermaid with fizzy red hair, her body a crescent moon.

Oh how I love to go up in the air, up in the air so high. When you fly you think you're growing, she marvels. *This is a nice vacation for you,* she says, as we fly along.

Everything up to now has been claustrophobia. All the jewels in Shockley's — rubies, sapphires, topazes — have gone to heaven and spread themselves across the sky like melting crayons. Transparencies of pale pink, alabaster, move around me, diaphanous, the negative of clouds. Creation is still happening. In outer space, in that superior air, they say there are colors we've never seen, the colors of electric shocks, as well as the enduring mauves.

The only work of humans you can see from outer space is a wall, Esther says.

A gull hovers next to me, startled, I'm startled, too — up here he is real; his feet are pink and he cries like a baby, breast feathers riffling in the wind.

Soon Esther and I are flying through a canyon of clouds, between steep walls of gray-violet, sheep-shaped clouds piled high. I melt into the fleece, and the clouds, three deep, lift like veils, turn a delicate pink, and disappear.

Down below, I am lying on the parachute. Shep is rubbing my feet, and everyone else is holding hands in a circle around me, eyes closed. Then one by one the strangers drift away from the circle. Grace cradles my head; Molly holds my hand. Bobby gets a sheaf of pampas grass from the truck, and he and Shep wave it over me.

How much easier it is to be nowhere — *now here* — nowhere on that unsteady earth. I can feel myself wanting to rise, higher, wanting to vanish like incense into the vault of heaven, but Esther is pulling me nearer to her, her hand firmly in mine.

Prayer is a ladder, she says loudly in my ear. *God makes the universe at every minute; we keep praying to keep Him interested. I sat up high in shul. The Yiddish theater too. I never got used to the shilly-shally flicker of the movies. Give me the stage, people standing on a real floor, their voices nice and loud. I hear voices, too. I hear your grandfather, Marx, Freud, Einstein, Rabbi Akiba, the great mystics Luria and Abulafia. Like in a crowded deli. With you it's the lightning — it turned you on like a radio. They're saying, 'Stop potchkeeing around! Wake up!'*

A cupcake-shaped cloud flies by and separates us for a second. *The sky is too much without a cloud,* Esther says. *You know about this,* she says. *We are pieces of the earth.* And then everything is in close-up, like in a movie. I see a lone gull disappearing in the folds of a splash, and Dove sitting on her red folding chair and fiddling with her shoe, entranced by the pure potential of untied laces.

Esther calls to her, and Dove looks up, the jelly-bean yellow aura around her turning to a soft fuzzy blue like a child's slippers. *I need to talk to her,* Esther confides, flying next to me now.

You're in my song, if only you have the patience, Esther half-sings to Dove. *Remembering is our tradition. Many Jews were shepherds in our early wanderings, as were our fathers in ancient days until we became unwelcome strangers. The walls of Jerusalem broken in many places. We who had been exiles in Babylon. This is your heirloom. Prophecy, tropes of fire. Tongues of angels, birds of God. After the year seventy we became a people without a home. Here's something to think about: What is a Holy Book? The Torah, inscribed on parchment, is our Holy Word. But the shepherds of that sheepskin became the scapegoats. Later we turned to farming. Continued hardship made us unhappy. We must remember, but thank God we can forget. The Jewish Quarter is rubble, all weeds and chickens clucking over the ruins, the fallen doors and stones somewhere in three dimensions which is history. A story you can tell me would touch me all the way to my heart. The Messiah will never come. His business is not to arrive but to be expected, which is good. From up here, I can see your father, whose grandfather was a Jew, dry goods, needles and thread, buttons and lace. Mazel tov, Dove. Jews and usury? We couldn't own land. No land to grow anything on! This is your heirloom. Later, you'll remember it out of nowhere.*

And Dove, thinking, *Come down here where the trees start,* goes back to tying her shoe.

We're getting closer, Esther says. She embraces me from behind, supporting my back, her hands over my abdomen. A warmth floods my body as I am held close. The heat from her body is immense. I am unaccountably happy. *You'll have all the time you'll ever need,* she says. *The sweet mysteries, di gantzeh megillah.* She kisses my cheek. *Ask the birds! Ask the trees!*

The earth is growing bigger and bigger as we cruise at lower and lower altitudes, bumping down the seven notes of Jacob's ladder, the atavistic octave. Everything around me is speeding fragments, but I feel as solid as a grandmother as I'm pulled by the *yoo-hoo* of the earth's magnetic field. For the first time in a long time, I have no fear.

To be fearless is to be heavenly, Esther says. *It's as refreshing as a fizzy beverage! Seltzer!* she says, her laughter falling as rapidly and deliriously as we are. *No fear! This, we call faith!* she croons as we hit the ground with a soft thud.

20

The garden in daylight is a miracle, an island in the midst of ruin. It's almost sunset, when the fragrance of spices marks the end of the Sabbath and you choose life all over again, a time when the colors are folded away like linens into the sky.

Molly is saying to Bobby and Grace, "Now, during a thunder-storm I'm like, get away from that pole! Get rid of those keys!" Bobby smiles a small smile, and Grace nods, absentmindedly smoothing her black T-shirt. I've told them how the faintest dab of gray ink in a cloud, the slightest puff of cumulonimbus, birds blowing like candy wrappers, and I used to lose my nerve, though now I think the fear has left me.

"When you felt the tremor you were probably remembering the lightning," Shep says. "Lightning craves the earth it's respon-sible for creating. That time it hit you it decided that you were the fastest way down. Something about you generated a strong electrical field."

"It's true," Molly says. "I break tape recorders all the time."

"Me too," I say. "Do you ever hear voices?"

"Come to think of it," she says.

Lightning sent the word of God through Moses, at Sinai, Esther says. *Light attracts light. The great rabbis, Hillel, Akiba, Mai-monides, were Trees of Life, no lightning could kill them, even when it sizzled straight through them, even when it split oaks like babies.*

"Just don't be the tallest thing," Shep continues. "Don't go looking to see what's wrong with anything. Don't talk on the telephone." He puts his arm around me. "You look changed."

I nod. It was different from fainting — leaving my body. I had fainted not long after the accidental conception, early in our marriage, some failure of the uterine wall. Then Michael and I decided that the earth had enough weight on it without more children. *Tsk,* Esther says.

Molly opens a thermos, pours tea into paper cups, and Shep hands them around. The tea has a deep-in-the-woods taste. We sit, quiet, as if we are sitting shivah. *Which means seven.* Dove crouches next to the rose bed, poking a small shovel into the earth with great concentration. The red hearts on top of her overall straps glow like rubies.

Esther hovers among us, untouched by gravity. *Tell Dove that Boris was deported to Siberia for his role in the nineteen-oh-five violins. Violence. Then later the Siege, the baby carriage.* Dove shakes her head like a cat with ear mites. "I'm digging to China," she announces, peering up at us.

Esther skims light from the trees as if she is clarifying a golden soup. *The Zaddiks say, remember your day backwards. I'm going backward from the thing I died of. Died of heart. Loved Joseph. Loved twins born, and Eleanore. My life.*

Leaf shapes of light shimmer in the dusk. "Esther! My darling dusklet!" I cry out. "Do you have somewhere else besides the earth?"

There is no answer. It is suddenly cold. I wrap my arms around myself and feel the onrush of darkness in the seemingly borderless garden. Havdalah. We are past the hour of sanctity. The night sky behind the day sky has appeared, the pure energy of the constellations winking down.

"I can name the consolations," Dove says, looking up. "The Big Dipper."

Molly laughs. "Put your jacket on, hon." Dove slips into a jacket with figures of drummers marching across the back. The sea air is moving in along with the evening. Blocks away, the seals are draped on Lighthouse Rock, the fog rolling in as soft as cashmere. At the ocean's dark edge there is a hem of white. Soon the moon's O will rise above us.

Esther is subsiding with each increment of darkness. *Look!* I hear her say, and I can see my grandfather waiting for her at his cigar store on Amsterdam Avenue, 1921, after the first war, standing under the OPTIMO cigar sign, wearing a three-piece suit, his hands clasped behind his back. Havanas, penny candy, toys at Christmas, pencils and homework books in September. A cat rubs against his legs, amiably indifferent to mice. *He fed it better than he fed himself,* Esther says, and then she recedes into a deeper distance where Boris also waits, in an astrakhan hat.

One more thing. She moves close now, her breath against my ear. *Next year put up a sukkah! Maybe you'll get married! So it won't be babies! God hears our beating hearts! God floats!* I see her face in the half-light from the chuppah that floats above her. 1910. *Too poor for bridesmaids.* She wears a simple ivory dress with a lace collar. The twins and Eleanore are there, and Dove, Molly, Shep, and me, everyone in her past and future.

"Don't go!" I cry out to her.

"Time to go," Molly says to Dove. But Dove stands like a sentry, unmoving, next to the hole she has dug.

"Don't go!" I call to Esther.

"C'mon, Dove," Shep says.

"Next time, sweetheart, we'll plant some bulbs," Bobby encourages.

"Some irises," Grace says.

Molly brushes the dirt off Dove's overalls. "That's not what she wants," she says, turning to us. "She just wants to see the light at the other end of the world." *She just wants to see the light at the other end of the world,* Esther explains, her voice overlapping with Molly's.

"Don't go!" I cry out to Esther, who is both near and far. Who will rescind her vanishing? She stays close to Dove while we gather our things and stack the crates in the corner of the garden. The ground under us moves a little, a barely perceptible shudder, and Esther sighs a canticle so faint I can barely hear its whisper — *Stay! Enjoy!* — as the earth shivers again, changes its mind, and saves itself for later.

Do You Know the Facts of Life? (Quiz)

SAMPLE QUESTION: *Did you ever, as an adolescent, want to kiss your own mouth in order to know how you felt to the people you were paired with randomly at parties, when the opposite sex still seemed as remote as Egypt? How many of you still want to kiss your own mouths?*

If you did well on the sample question, you'll want to take the rest of this exam. Sample answers are provided to the following questions in order to keep you company in your ruminations and to give you encouragement if you hesitate or stray. A final score will not be tallied in this quiz.

1. *We all know that the origins of sexuality are in the family. Write a brief essay about sex in your family.*

Her mother, when she's very little, informs her that babies come from seeds. She inspects every flowerpot in the house to see if a brother or sister is on its way. Later her mother liberally expands the information but keeps a strict eye on her growing daughter. In fact, because of her mother's watchfulness there are many episodes in the girl's childhood of *feelie interruptus*. Billy Emerson's boy's breath two inches away in a tantalizing almost. Games of doctor with little red pills and white caps. And her mother popping up like a doll out of a Swiss clock, always, at the sexiest moment, calling, "Hi, kids, milk and cookies!"

2. *What was your first sexual game?*

She is seven years old and she and Barbara Lombardi are on the porch with their clothes on playing a game they invented called Naked in Hell. They are pretending they have big firm shapely breasts like movie stars in 1940s sweaters but they are naked and in hell, where it is all right to be fiendishly wicked and naked. There is no narrative line in this game (which is invisible to anyone observing them); the point is to set the scene and then feel the tension of the naughtiness, to delight in hours of tumescence and then at dinnertime run into their houses to be little girls in the bosoms of their families. This is the same year that Lana Turner, according to a Hollywood exercise coach, had a perfect body for one week, and four years before Barbara is sexually approached in their neighborhood by a stranger the police fail to apprehend. By then they are eleven years old and she has to walk Barbara home if it's after dark because she's the brave and untouched one. But on the way back, alone, she makes her repel-the-attacker face, grimace of a Japanese actor, while inside of herself she chants, "I'm plain, I'm plain, don't hurt me, don't hurt me," over and over, until she has reached the warm and extended light of her mother's window.

3. *Write an essay on sex and school.*

Richard Krebs, the sixth-grade bully, tells her he can see her when she takes a shower. Although she knows this is impossible, she thinks he may have some apparatus, the kind boys invent and girls don't, that will allow him to see her, so she takes faster and faster showers. Then, apparently overnight, Jerry Smith turns from good boy into dirty joker. "How far is the Old Log Inn? Yuk yuk." She doesn't like the coarseness of the jokes, though she does

enjoy the secrecy the jokes are told in. On the way home from
school the girls run away from the boys so they can be caught
(additional question: *When did* your *cleverness begin?*) and she
looks forward to that from lunchtime until three p.m. One day
Michael Garrison spreads the rumor that he saw under her skirt
when it flew up, but she knows he didn't because he didn't men-
tion the "Tuesday" embroidered in red against white cotton over
her appendix. In any case, taunts are compliments in those early
days, and the girls thrill to them because they are a sign of interest, an advance over being shunned. This is where confusion begins, and these divisions are reflected, finely honed, even in her
recent dreams.

4. *Relate a recent sexual dream, or several recent sexual dreams.*
    She has had two sexual dreams this week, one tantric and
one horrific. In the tantric one she's sitting in the archaeologi-
calligraphy cafe with her lover, the sunshine streaming in on
ferns and oak tables. There are ancient runes on the walls, the
braille of shadows and light. She and her lover finger the runes
for sexual instructions, which are instantly translated by their
bodies into their bodies. In the horrific dream a karate expert
chews up pieces of wood until he has crammed his mouth full of
splinters. Then he leans forward to kiss her. She wakes up.

5. *Now see what connections exist between sex and sleep.*
    She and her lover spend many days in bed   making love
eating leftover Chinese food   playing backgammon   eating
pizza   making love   watching Busby Berkeley and *Black
Orpheus* on black and white TV he tells her the colors   five
days go by and he says, "Are you really going all the way into the
kitchen? Let me go with you"   reading her Zippy and *King
Lear*   playing guitar   it is summer   sultry   a scrim of
leaves outside the window   they are singing endless duets of

scat invented on the spot   they make up a pastime called
Scenes You Never Saw writing the erotic passages left out of the
great novels   they relinquish themselves to the heat   by
accident he knocks her earrings off in his passion   it's all she
wears   he always finds them again and places them in her
palm   they worry they'll forget how to buy food   go to the
bank   read a book   call a friend   you put your forefin-
ger in he says and dial   and *then* what she says   they say
hello he says   and then what   their legs are gently pret-
zeled   they can't get up they giggle they need a servant   they
are starving to death   their bodies ache   maggots are in
the garbage hairs in the sink the daily papers accumulate at the
door of the clapboard house   the air-conditioning's breaking
down his spinster cousin whose bed they are in comes back from
vacation after they've gone and finds it clean but she has insomnia every night for a whole year.

6. *Explore the relationship between sex and insomnia.*
    She has insomnia, so she's watching the Johnny Carson show.
A comedienne is on, horse faced, skinny, and funny. She was
making love with her husband, the comedienne says, when he
said, "Say something dirty." She was immediately responsive:
"The bathroom," she said, "the kitchen, the living room, the
playroom." While she watches TV she thumbs through a paper-
back someone left behind, *The Coming Celibacy.* Edward, eight
months celibate, says, "I'm much more sensitive to things now.
For example, I can hear a lot better if there's something wrong
with my car." On screen two puppets are enacting an adultery
scene, the wife at home is being visited by the milkman. "I can't
open the door in my underwear," she says. "You have a door in
your underwear?" the milkman replies. "Let me in and I'll help
you open it."

7. Interview one or two of your friends on the subject of underwear.

"I really like it," says Andrea, putting her feet up on the coffee table. "My all-time favorites were crimson silk with eggshell lace to be seductive for Ted before things got bad between us, then I gave up and wore flannel and wool. Girdles? I did wear a girdle for forty minutes in Shiraz. I had gotten really fat on pistachio nuts and could not get into this blue silk dress and Mother and Dad had to push me into her girdle minutes before the ambassador's party and then I got a stomachache and had to go home and never wore one again."

While talking to Andrea she remembers her honeymoon in Paris, where a friend had warned her about a flourishing white slave trade in lingerie shops: Middlemen would snatch you from the cubicle where you were trying on your *soutien-gorge* and sell you into a bordello in the Sahara. She was twenty, her fingers trembling; she fastened the garter belt made of slender strips of lace as her husband stood guard outside, the way he stood guard at the famous hairdresser's, keeping him from cutting more than an inch of her waist-length hair, the hair that was so often praised by the artists she posed for back in New York.

8. Have you ever posed in the nude?

She works as a model for a few serious New York artists and occasionally for a commercial artist. One night the commercial artist does a series of drawings he hopes to sell to *Playboy* of her reaching, twisting, dreaming into space, all very beautiful, really. It's nighttime, his studio is on the twentieth floor of an office building, luxe and quiet; dead cameras standing around on tripods, two enormous drawing boards, Cartier-Bresson photographs on the walls, humanized hi-tech. Every time she takes a new pose he says, "Great! Great!" It is a strange experience to know that he sees far more in her than what, at that moment, she feels in herself. This, she realizes later, is exactly what it means to be an object. As he keeps busy with pad and charcoal, it frees her to drift and dream. She stares for ten minutes at the face of a Russian woman in one of the photographs until she feels herself lift into an enlightenment she has never felt before. Years later she understands that even meditation has not given her that sense of stillness and of clarity. The artists are not predatory but, on the contrary, protective and fatherly. She feels the air on her naked body as they sketch an image of her onto the soft stretched canvas, and it is as if she is three years old and playing at the shore while her parents sit close by, laughing and eating sandwiches but keeping an eye on her, building her sense of who she is just by being there.

9. *Have you ever posed in the nude with your clothes on?*
He photographs her face while she's telling him a subtly erotic story. It looks like an ordinary picture when it's developed but it excites him every time he looks at it.

10. *Have you ever attended a pornographic movie?*
She and her husband are parting, a marriage of many years begun in Paris and ending in California, and spend their last evening together at the movies, a common practice among divorcing couples. With a sense of fitness and of humor they attend the program of historical comic erotic movies at the local art cinema, and her annoyance with the banality of those bodies using each other without emotion wins out over her terror and delight in seeing so much active flesh. At the break before the feature an attractive man sits down in the empty seat on her right. Her husband has left in order to go to the men's room. She asks the man if he saw the shorts. "No," he says, he came for the feature. "They were stupefying," she says. It is clear that he enjoys her use of the word *stupefying* and she enjoys his enjoyment of it.

They chat a little. Her husband comes back and he and the man exchange mild but indescribable looks. When the lights go out she feels how fully the man fills his seat, and she leans slightly closer to him than to her husband as a symbol of her new life as distinguished from her old. The man moves a fraction closer, and she feels the density of the muscles of his upper arm next to hers. The entire movie is spent adjusting these fractions closer and closer, allowing them to be background to the film and then foreground, eclipsing the film, until at a certain point she and the man simultaneously feel a need to rest, and withdraw, like two sweaty people flung apart to cool after making love. She is surprised at how merry and comforted she feels: He has a solid body; it is very nice. She does not, however, have fantasies that involve sex with strangers. If she'd wanted to be anonymous, she wouldn't have said *stupefying* after all, a word that would set her apart from other people, especially in California.

Reflect on your answers to the questions above and take a ten-minute break.

Begin again with some short answers:

11. *What is the opposite of an obscene phone call?*
It's a call where you breathe gently, surprise them with kindness, and hang up. A good thing to say is, "Everything you've done up to now has been just fine with me," or "You too will love again."

12. *What is your favorite advice-to-the-lovelorn column?*
She reads in Ann Landers's column a query it will take her at least twenty years to comprehend. "I'm worried," says the correspondent, "because I am pregnant by a man who has slept with so many women I cannot be sure he is the father of my baby."

13. *Now, at your leisure, notice what sexual associations cling to the objects that surround you. Or close your eyes and remember other objects and places you have, at some time in your life, charged with eros.*

Memory is itself sexual, a Dionysian attachment to the past accomplished in the face of the scythings of Father Time. She closes her eyes and thinks of: nude beaches; the skin of birches; surfers taking a wave that will never return; damp heaps of russet leaves; *keep cooking till chicken falls off fork;* a willow tree that sinks to its knees as the light subsides; a chemise with green flowers swaying into ivory like the pattern on her grandmother's fine Victorian china, a pattern he liked, the edge of her hand in his mouth, the woods all around, half in darkness, then later the two of them spilled open like loosened yarn or the day she met him in winter sun she said my hands, they're cold, and he took them between his own steepled fingers, the delicious prestige of a first gesture.

Now take a twenty-minute break. During the break, lie down, close your eyes, and imagine your own nakedness. Then, using only your imagination, paint your body until you are covered from the soles of your feet all the way up through your hair. Apply whatever colors seem right to you, by whatever means. When you are finished, lie quietly for a few minutes.

14. *Having relaxed yourself completely, write an essay that is also a confession.*

A year before the divorce and after long consideration she took a lover — not the usual adultery (guilt, repentance, the stunned mate) but a passion undertaken with her husband's tacit consent. In spite of the consent, whenever her lover called she pulled the phone on its long cord into the walk-in closet and sat among the dresses and skirts and trousers to mute her conversation and to find the privacy she did not want her husband's voice, deep in her head, to encroach upon. Her husband had a suit he liked, a Pierre Cardin that hung in a zippered cover next to where she leaned against the wall to talk on the phone, and she would look abstractedly at the silvery printing on the case, CAR DIN, and think about the rush of traffic outside the hotel where she had last met her lover, and about the novel and graceful allegiances of his golden dreamy body. She would talk to him for hours and emerge from the closet dizzy with the murmur of their voices folded over one another, letting the murmuring seep into her as she lay on the bed in a stupor. One day she reached for her coat in the closet and realized that her dizziness was caused not by her lover's voice but by the mothballs nestled in her husband's suit, their cold insulting sweetness even now seeping into her nostrils and numbing her slightly. Her husband's cleverly accidental control of her while she talked to her lover made her feel she was losing the last of her power, and she decided finally that the marriage was over. The day she packed her bags, a month after she had broken up with her lover because it would be dishonorable to abandon one man simply to go to another, she scooped the mothballs out of the zippered case and replaced them with a dozen candy Easter eggs she had bought that morning at Woolworth's when she was buying her luggage tags. She neatly arranged the yellow and violet eggs under the knife-creased and impeccably silent suit. And then she bit a hole in it.

15. *Follow this confession with a consideration of the spiritual side of things. What real or imagined encounters have you had with sex gods or goddesses?*

It's November 1, All Souls' Day, the day, she thinks to herself, that the dead come back in the form of candy. She's at the local sweet shop, eating chocolate because she's lonely, when suddenly a vision appears. She always hallucinates a little if she eats a lot of chocolate and today she sees a woman in a preshrunk pink punk T-shirt and sheepskin chaps with a banner across her chest that says SEX GODDESS except the S seems to have fallen off. "I'm on a lecture tour," the goddess says. "I talk about how in the fifties people lay together like flounders and flopped up and down. In the sixties sex was based on political values; polygamy echoed communal action. In the eighties everyone carries the burden alone. So promiscuity — from which the word *prom* was taken — is —"

At the word *prom* a taffeta gown materializes, with a pretty woman in it. "This is Pam," the goddess says, "former prom queen and pom-pom girl."

"Hiya," Pam says, "I hear you're getting divorced. Well honey, you're gonna be lonely. Eat that chocolate. How will you ever live without a man, and I'm telling you, the men out there are all too young, too mean, or married. You'll be singing the blues," she says, and she sashays out humming an old tune in 4/4 time, "If you don't like my sweet potato, why did you dig so deep?" The ex-goddess shrugs and, shrugging, vanishes, chaps first.

16. *Write an essay on sex and solitude.*

She decides to prove the prom queen wrong and proceeds to lead a balanced and ascetic life, no chocolate. After several months of this, however, she suddenly loses her tranquillity to lust that her laws against the young, the mean, and the married will not allow her to satisfy. The man dazzles her — red satin flash and life in the f-lane, twenty-four hours a day. Why does she always fall for actors and musicians, the strutting mimes and mummers, the bragging drummers, men dependent on the vulgarisms of amps and artificial lights, when she should be drawn to sonnets and starlight? Violations of good taste have such appeal for her that she wonders whether desire is only a state of disorientation, a matter of breaking sober habits so deeply ingrained that their very disruption seems erotic.

She falls into a state of sexual dyslexia: Reading the Bible for courage, she understands it to say that Job is afflicted with sore balls; taking her minerals in the morning, she finds a sodomite on the label where dolomite should be. Hours are lost in fantasy. Finally she imagines going to visit Herbal Cowboy, a healer, making a long trek through the redwoods, home of hippie witches in their covens hovering over their ovens and caldrons, to his shack in the mountains, where he mixes a concoction and writes a prescription. Her cure, he says, lies in dreaming the same dream night after night, a dream in which she is scrubbing down the steps of the Philadelphia Museum of Art. Eventually the lust will disappear, provided she avoids looking inside the museum — the Kandinskys have a certain bright diaphanous thrust and shatter that might disturb. He also gives her a pass to Wet World, where, having misread "groupers" as "gropers" and then as "groupies" on the giant fish-tank plaque, she decides to soothe herself with mammals instead.

She stands at the rim of the porpoise pool and one of the porpoises surfaces and puts his head close to her hand. She strokes his head and his back: It's like petting a giant olive. Intelligence always arouses her sexually, and the porpoise is no exception. She looks into his little eyes and feels herself getting turned on by his brain capacity. The porpoise is attracted by the sheen and shimmer of the satin cowboy shirt she is wearing, and he inches closer, his long nose touching her waist, as if he understands her human silliness and shine. She envisions how lovely it would be to swim with him, speaking in whistles and rusty hinge noises, clicks and pingings reverberating through her whole being, touch and sound indistinguishable in the echolalia as they plunge again and again below the mirror of silver waves.

After a day of these fantasies she goes to sleep and she dreams, not about the flashy man who inspired her lust but about the porpoise. He speaks to her in playful swoops of freshness and rebounds of shyness, his body saying, "Swim with me! Swim with me!" As they swim, the water brilliant and quiet, he nuzzles her, the dark blue depths widening under them. And then, in the voice of a creature who now, involved, fears their differences, who cannot cross a border without vanishing, he says, "Let me go, for the day breaketh," and she lets him go, instantly, and wakes up feeling very clear, her eyes full of tears.

17. *You have almost finished the exam. Conclude it by sitting quietly in a lotus position. Close your eyes and contemplate the ten thousand sensuous things in the physical world. Don't tally your score.*

Notice the white throat of an iris, the quiver of emerald hummingbirds, the rolling gold hills of California summer studded with live oaks. (*What do you consider the most voluptuous season? Don't rest with the obvious. Maybe it's the late yielding light of autumn, the intimacy in that clarity, the sharpness of light that brings everything closer.*) Consider the texture of thin silk velvet, consider the scent of star jasmine, Billie Holiday's voice, any serious tenor saxophonist playing "Body and Soul," Edward Weston's nudes. Georgia O'Keeffe's orchids and lilies. Consider your childhood, the shapes of light in the room, the attentions and rhythms of speech, the fluxes and cuttings, the touch. This is the paradise where generosity begins. Swim with me, swim with me. These are the facts of life. Now, come to your senses.